REQUIEM
❧ FOR A ❧
REALTOR

REQUIEM
❧ FOR A ❧
REALTOR

A Father Dowling Mystery

Ralph McInerny

St. Martin's Minotaur
New York

www.minotaurbooks.com

ISBN 0-312-32417-0
EAN 978-0312-32417-9

First Edition: July 2004

10 9 8 7 6 5 4 3 2 1

To John and
Mary O'Callaghan

❧ Part One ❧

Although Marie Murkin, housekeeper of the St. Hilary rectory, regarded others her age as old, she still thought of herself as young. Well, younger. She dismissed her aches and pains as temporary anomalies, not evidence that time's creaking chariot was catching up to her. The fact that she was childless was a partial explanation of her attitude. In their children, parents have ever before their eyes a measure of their passage through this vale of tears, but Marie, like the celibates she had cared for, had no such reminders.

Abandoned by her husband, a ne'er-do-well sailor who had returned after years of absence only to die, she had unconsciously developed a somewhat cynical attitude toward marriage and family life. And, of course, in a rectory, one tended to see the failures rather than the successes. For all that, Marie had no negative premonitions when Stanley Collins showed up at the rectory door and asked to see Father Dowling.

"I'm not a parishioner."

"You're new in the parish?"

"I used to live in St. Hilary's. As a kid."

Marie had come to see herself as the filter through which only worthy callers on the pastor could pass. This visitor had much to commend him. He was a handsome man, tall, broad of chest, an interesting face dominated by a mouth that wore a disarming smile. His deference to her stood him in good stead.

"Father hasn't returned yet from his noon Mass."

"I suppose I should have telephoned first."

Marie led him into the front parlor and indicated a chair for him to sit in. The absence of the pastor gave her an excellent opportunity to grill the visitor.

"Did you mention your name?"

"Stanley Collins."

"There were Collins in the parish."

"On Lincoln Avenue. My parents."

"Ah."

"I have been told that Father Dowling is a canon lawyer."

"That's right."

"And he served on the archdiocesan marriage court?"

"That was before his appointment to St. Hilary's. You want to consult him as a canon lawyer?"

"You're the housekeeper?"

"I am." Marie's tone suggested that this title did not begin to tell the story of her role in the rectory. "And have been for many years." She cleared her throat. "I have been here longer than the pastor."

"There were Franciscans here when my parents lived in the parish."

"Yes." This was a sore point with Marie. She had come into her position when the Franciscans were in charge, and she had found them difficult to bring to heel, despite the sandals they wore. *Il Poverello* would have had difficulty recognizing the clerics who bore his name. A succession of friars had characterized Marie's first years at St. Hilary's, and she had seriously thought of resigning when suddenly, as it seemed, the Franciscan hegemony ended and Father Roger Dowling arrived as pastor. With him she had worked out a modus vivendi that seemed satisfying on both sides. Not that he always appreciated the pastoral help she gave him.

"When will Father Dowling be back?"

"Oh, we have time."

He seemed surprised.

"Perhaps you could give me some idea of why you want to see Father."

The sound of the kitchen door opening and closing brought Marie swiftly to her feet. The key to her effectiveness was to conceal the role she played.

"There he is! Wait here."

She scurried down the hall and stopped Father Dowling as he came into the dining room. "There's someone to see you."

"Oh?" He was tall and thin with a prominent nose, and his eyes softened what would otherwise have seemed an austere countenance. "Who is it?"

"Lunch is ready. I'll ask him to wait."

"Nonsense." He went past her, looked into his study, and then continued on to the front parlor. An exchange of greetings and then, as she might have predicted, he issued an invitation to join him for lunch. Good. Now she could listen in as they talked over their meal.

2

Lunch was salad and *saltimbocca alla romana.* Father Dowling was glad to see his guest tuck into it, rolling his eyes in appreciation at the first taste of the veal. Marie had hesitated before disappearing into the kitchen, hands beneath her apron. She knew better than to expect an adequate reaction to her cooking from the pastor who ate whatever was put before him and thought that like God in Genesis, anything she made was good, but the man who had identified himself as Stanley Collins might have been awarding her a *cordon bleu* then and there.

"This is better than any I have ever had."

Marie did not exactly giggle, but she went through the swinging door into her kitchen, a woman fulfilled.

"You understand I'm not a parishioner, Father."

"We have a few openings left."

Collins laughed. "I did live in St. Hilary's as a kid. My parents lived and died here. As I told Mrs. Murkin."

Father Dowling's eyebrows rose. "I hope you didn't have to wait long for me to return."

A shrug. "Ten, fifteen minutes. I should have called. I had no idea I would be treated so royally. The reason I came—"

Father Dowling held up a hand. "Enjoy your lunch. We can talk afterward in my study."

Did the silence in the kitchen alter? Father Dowling had no doubt that Marie was on sentry duty. Perhaps he should have been more annoyed at her nosiness than he was, but as often as not it helped that Marie kept herself au courant on parish business. Not that he would ever tell her that. Nor of course did he want to convey to Stanley Collins that he was criticizing Marie.

"I am told you are a canon lawyer, Father," Collins said when they were settled in the study. The lingering aroma of tobacco seemed to surprise him. He watched with wonder as Father Dowling filled his pipe.

"I hope you're not bothered by smoke?"

"Good God, no. Could I have a cigarette?"

"I can't offer you one."

But Collins had extracted a package from his jacket pocket. He leaned over the desk to light it on Father Dowling's match and sat waiting until the pastor had succeeded in getting his pipe going to his satisfaction.

"You were on the archdiocesan marriage court, Father?"

"A long time ago. Or so it seems."

Had Collins come here for advice on an annulment? The very thought filled Father Dowling with unwelcome memories of the bleak years during which he had processed requests for recognition that a marriage had not occurred. In those days, it had been far more difficult to prove such a claim.

"You understand I am no longer on the tribunal."

Collins nodded. How much did he know of Roger Dowling's ignominious departure from the tribunal? For a moment, the pastor was overwhelmed by the contrast between his former duties and his life at St. Hilary's.

"My wife is having an affair, Father."

Collins's cheerful expression was gone. Had he come to confess his wife's sins?

"That's not cause for an annulment, Mr. Collins."

"Annulment! I don't want an annulment." His look of gloom returned. "My wife says we're not really married."

"Tell me about it," Father Dowling said, trying to keep resignation out of his voice.

Stanley Collins and his wife Phyllis had not been married in the Church. They had avoided a Catholic wedding on the advice of a priest who seemed to think that they should not bind themselves so completely until they were sure. This sort of bad advice was all too frequently given of late, in good faith, perhaps, though Father Dowling lamented it. When marriage was regarded as a temporary experiment that is what it too often proved to be. The Collinses had been married in a civil ceremony in Evanston ten years ago, and until quite recently everything had gone smoothly.

"You never thought of getting your marriage blessed?"

"I wish I had! Now Phyllis says she is in love with another man, and she wants a divorce so she can marry him in the Church."

Life without law would be impossible, but it was not always much better with it. The intricacies of the marriage code were many, and the Church's attitude toward annulment had seemed to blur of late.

"Can she do that, Father?"

"I would have to know more than I do," he said with the sinking realization that this invited Collins to go on in the expectation that something more than mere advice would be forthcoming.

"I suppose I have pretty much kept my nose to the grindstone." Collins was a Realtor, in partnership with a man named

George Sawyer, a college friend. "We've done pretty well. I always thought I was doing it for Phyllis, and now she complains that I neglected her."

"Children?"

He shook his head, and his eyes drifted along a shelf of books. "We thought we'd wait."

Until they had their marriage blessed? Perhaps that, too, had been part of the advice they had been given. Despite himself, Father Dowling was thinking of ways he might shunt Collins on to someone else. But who? There was no point in sending him to the marriage tribunal. There he would be told that his wife could divorce him and, in the present state of affairs, could doubtless have a Church wedding all in white with her lover. He could imagine how all this would seem to Collins: the Church siding with his wife and colluding in the breakup of his marriage.

"Would it help if I talked with her?"

"I wish you'd talk to him."

Father Dowling waited. He would not ask for the man's name.

"You know him."

"I do?"

"Jameson. David Jameson."

Father Dowling took the pipe from his mouth. Jameson! "You're sure?"

"I am sure. Phyllis makes no bones about it. He's a dentist and she seems to think she's trading up."

When in doubt, review what has already been said. Father Dowling had Collins go over and over what he had already told him, he himself added a number of irrelevancies about the marriage tribunal, got his pipe going again, and perhaps managed to conceal the surprise the mention of David Jameson had given him.

Jameson's dental practice had prospered, and he was a prominent parishioner and a frequent presence at the rectory. The last time they had talked, Jameson had inquired about the possibility of becoming a permanent deacon. He was to all appearances a pillar of the church.

"How far have things gone with your wife and Jameson?"

"All the way."

No need to pursue that. The phrase left little doubt. Father Dowling had no inclination to ask Collins how he had come by his certainty.

"Will you talk to him, Father?" Collins asked.

"Would your wife come here?"

"Father, she says they plan to be married here."

Marie kept her mouth shut when David Jameson was on the scene, literally. She always felt he was examining her teeth when she talked. Among her vanities was the conviction that no one could possibly tell that she wore dentures, but how could you fool a dentist? His manner toward her should have won her heart. He was deferential, flattering, attentive, the soul of courtesy. Yet Marie did not trust his sincerity. Besides, he was what her late and unlamented husband would have called a Holy Joe.

It was a bitter truth that Father Dowling seemed to like Jameson. He appeared happy to see the dentist whenever he dropped in, gave him all the time he wanted when he did, and accompanied him to the door when he left. Just before leaving, Jameson would ask for Father Dowling's blessing.

Watching the gangly dentist bow his head as Father Dowling murmured the formula and made the sign of the cross over him, Marie could have growled. The first time he had done that, he had been about to kneel, but Father Dowling stopped him. On this Wednesday afternoon, Father Dowling closed the door on Jameson and turned to see Marie before she could slip away. Or maybe she wanted him to see her.

"Did he just leave?"

"He?"

"You know who. I thought dentists had to work."

"Not on Wednesdays. At least in his case. Did you want to make an appointment?"

She just looked at him. It was dangerous to think she could best him in banter.

"Why isn't he married?"

"Marie, I had no idea. Does he?"

"Idea of what?"

"Your secret passion, of course. Maybe making an appointment at his office would be a way to break the ice."

A special place in heaven awaited the housekeeper who could take the teasing of a pastor in submissive silence. She waited him out for half a minute.

"Or I could ask him to come to lunch some Wednesday . . ."

"You know I can't stand him."

"I'm told that is the form it sometimes takes."

"How many visitors ask for your blessing every time they leave?"

"I know, I know. But we mustn't criticize. Perhaps Dr. Jameson's example will bring back the practice."

"Maybe he has a vocation."

"That *would* be an impediment," he said, after a pause.

Marie gave up and stormed back to her kitchen where she made a pot of tea and sat, ready to polish it off unaided when Father Dowling pushed through the swinging door.

"Marie, I want to tap your formidable memory."

She looked at him warily.

"Do you recall the Stanley Collins who was here on Monday?"

"What about him?"

"That is my question to you."

He pulled out a chair and sat across the table from her. There was no point in offering him tea.

"I'll make coffee."

"Let me have half a cup of tea."

This was a surprise. He hated tea. She poured him a full cup and when she sat again pushed the plate of tollhouse cookies toward him.

"Stanley Collins," she began.

Sometimes her memory frightened Marie. Things you had no idea you were picking up stuck in the mind, and when one came out, others followed, clinging to it the way paper clips cling to a magnet, one after the other, a whole chain, as if everything was connected with everything else.

The Collinses who would have been Stanley's parents had married late, he a childless widower, she a woman on the shady side of thirty who might have been ready to throw in her cards when Frederick Collins made a bid for her hand. She was a teller in the bank where he was a vice president, a terminal post but a respectable one. He wore a suit seven days a week and had no recreation other than feeding the ducks in the park. He was lonely, of course, but so was she. She taught him to play cribbage, and one thing led to another. She must have been in her mid-thirties when they married, and a year later she had Stanley. An only child, they spoiled him rotten; he went to a military high school and off to Marquette for college. Summers he had been in camp, first as a camper, then as a counselor. He wasn't much companionship for his parents, but perhaps they preferred it that way. And they could not have been exhilarating company for him.

"He must have inherited a good amount when they died."

"When was that?"

Marie waved a hand. "I'd have to look it up. A long time ago. A tragic accident. One winter day, they were warming up the car in a closed garage and were asphyxiated."

"Good heavens."

"It's not what you think. They were on their way to Mass. Their missals were between them on the front seat."

"I wonder if Stanley had married by then."

Something clicked in Marie's mind. "Fifteen years ago. It was the last funeral Father Pacific ever conducted. A double."

"Pacific?"

"I know. And his family name was Hug."

"How do you remember all these things?"

"Some things are hard to forget."

"Why did you say their son would have inherited a lot of money?"

"Mr. Cadbury could tell you about that. He was a trustee of the bank where Collins worked."

"And he confided in you?"

"Of course not!" Why did he always have to spoil things, and just when they were having the kind of consultation Marie thought should be more frequent?

"Then how do you know?"

"It must have been in the paper."

He tipped his head in disbelief.

"Father, some things you just know and you don't know where you got them."

He accepted that. Good thing. She would never admit what she had just remembered. She had wheedled it out of Maud, Mr. Cadbury's jill of all trades at his law office. Since those days, Maud had become a bitter enemy who resented her employer's paeans of praise for Marie's culinary magic.

4

David Jameson's latest visit had been a trial. All the while they talked, Father Dowling was remembering Stanley Collins's accusation, and it was difficult not to try to imagine Jameson in the role of illicit lover. Whether or not the lady was married, 'going all the way' with her was hardly the behavior one expected of someone asking how he might begin training for ordination as a permanent deacon. Permanent deacons were not celibate, but they were bound by the sixth and ninth commandments like everybody else.

"In high school I thought of the priesthood."

"That's not unusual."

"I don't mean daydreams. I wrote to any number of religious orders. I still have the materials they sent. Oh, I suppose there was fantasizing involved. I would moon over their brochures, study the schedule of their seminarians, imagine myself in the role."

"It never went beyond that?"

"I familiarized myself with the curriculum of the major semi-nary later. I bought the textbooks for philosophy and theology and read them all. Canon law, too."

"Why didn't you enter the seminary?"

"I was destined for dental school from birth."

"Before your baby teeth?"

No point in jesting with David Jameson. His mind was literal and without humor. Another impediment to imagining him as illicit lover. "I was meant to fulfill my father's dream."

"He wanted to be a dentist?"

"In the worst way. But he was a barber and that was that. When fluoride seemed to eradicate cavities, he wavered, but then he read an article about the boom in orthodontics."

"Straightening teeth?"

"Improving your smile, is the way we put it."

"So you're an orthodontist?"

"At first. I've moved into dental surgery. We used to send people to specialists for root canals. Now we can do them ourselves. That's my speciality."

"Root canals?"

"You know what they are?"

"Sufficiently."

"It is quite lucrative. The market economy reigns in dentistry. Up to a point. Many of my patients are on dental plans, and limits are set."

"Ah."

"Even so." Jameson's eyes drifted away. "It is not a fulfilling life, Father."

"Not many cavities?"

Careful, careful. But Jameson was pursuing his own thoughts.

"When I come here to talk to you I get a sense of what my life might have been. I have a recurrent bad dream that when I die

I'll come before St. Peter and learn that I really did have a religious vocation. And I wasted my life doing root canals."

"God is merciful."

He knew that Marie Murkin regarded Jameson as a sanctimonious ass, and a case could be made for that judgment. But sanctimonious asses had souls, too.

"And it's not too late, David. How old are you?"

"I'll be forty my next birthday."

"There are seminaries for delayed vocations. For that matter, most vocations are delayed nowadays."

Jameson looked wistful. "You make me feel like those people in the parable who had an excuse for declining the invitation to the wedding."

"You never married?"

"No."

"Surely you must have thought of it."

This was sailing close to the wind, but it seemed to emerge naturally from the conversation.

"Oh, I suppose everyone does." He stopped. "I mean lay people."

"It's the normal course of life."

"Life gets into choppy waters sometimes."

"So you have thought of it?"

"Some day I will tell you all about it, Father. Maybe sooner rather than later."

"I look forward to that."

Jameson hesitated, as if sooner had come sooner than he expected. But he remained silent.

"Of course permanent deacons can marry."

Jameson brightened. "That's what got my mind going on it." His smile dimmed. "But what if it is a temptation? What if I am turning away from what I ought to be?"

Father Dowling had not met many cases of true scrupulosity, and he doubted that David Jameson was one of them. However devoid in imagination and humor, the dentist obviously enjoyed agonizing over the road not taken. Maybe his vocation was imagining he had a vocation. The subject of the permanent diaconate seemed to have been sidelined, which was all right with Father Dowling. He was not a fan of permanent deacons. He had never met a bishop who was. Yet they kept ordaining them. Not as many as formerly, but what was the point? What was needed was more priests. Or housekeepers like Marie Murkin.

Two hours later there was a pastoral twinkle in Marie's eye when she stuck her head into the study and said, "Phyllis Collins to see you."

Before closing the study door, Marie gave Phyllis Collins the once-over, and it was pretty clear that the visitor had failed some test.

"If tobacco smoke bothers you we can sit in the front parlor," Father Dowling said, still standing.

"Oh, I'm used to it. My husband smokes." She settled into her chair, began to cross her legs, then thought better of it.

She must be forty, but she dressed like a girl. A dangerously short skirt with corresponding decolletage and her hair, worn long, was of several colors, brunette streaked with blonde. She raked it with the painted fingers of one hand. "David Jameson suggested I talk with you."

"I see."

"He has been a great help to me of late." Her voice quavered and she seemed about to cry. Father Dowling wished he had taken her to the front parlor, or that Marie had left the door open.

"My husband is unfaithful, Father. He has been running around for years."

He adopted an appropriate expression, but, of course, her words confused him. Stanley Collins had sat in that same chair and accused his wife of having an affair with Jameson, but now Phyllis Collins was telling him that her husband was a womanizer.

"We weren't married in the Church, Father."

"Why not?"

"Stanley talked me out of it. What a fool I was. Or, at least, that is what I've come to think."

"You've changed your mind?"

"Is it true that a civil marriage doesn't count?"

"Of course it counts. But not in the way a sacramental marriage does."

"But even they get dissolved, don't they?"

"You want to dissolve your marriage?"

She sat back in shock. "No! Stanley does. He has fallen in love with some tramp and wants to leave me for her."

It was tempting to tell her of Stanley's visit, but doubtless she would counter with what she had already said. Had Stanley's visit been a preemptive strike?

"My big mistake was telling him what David told me."

"Jameson?"

She nodded. "About Church law. He knows all about it."

Father Dowling said nothing. There was no canon law against lay people reading the code of canon law, and they could talk about what they read, why not? But it sounded as if David Jameson was impersonating a canon lawyer.

"I gather he's a friend of yours," he said.

"He's my dentist."

"Then he can't be a friend."

Perhaps ten seconds went by before she smiled. Did her smile owe something to Dr. Jameson's skills? "Oh, he's a friend, too. I don't know why I began to confide in him about Stanley. But he wasn't a friend then, just a dentist." Another smile. "He was explaining an X-ray to me, showing me why I didn't need a root canal, and suddenly I burst into tears. What was the point of trying to keep my looks if my husband didn't care?"

Her words evoked a tender scene. She supine in the dental chair, a bib under her chin to guard against drooling and perhaps concupiscence as well, David Jameson in his pale green dentist coat, holding the X-ray to the light, and suddenly she is in tears. Not an ideal spot for a dentist to be in, a sobbing woman in his chair, her pain obviously more emotional than physical. It seemed extenuating. Jameson's comforting, at least initially, might have been prompted by professional panic. For that matter, Phyllis Collins's manner of dress and the streaked hair and the rest of it might be part of a pathetic effort to keep her husband.

"And you became friends?"

She nodded. "I could talk to David. Relatives, women friends, I just couldn't bring myself to tell them about Stanley. My mother never really forgave me for not marrying in the Church. And my brother Bob always hated Stanley."

"Does he live in town?"

He did. Bob Oliver.

"And Dr. Jameson told you about canon law?"

"And I, like a fool, told Stanley. But two can play at that game, can't they? If we were divorced I could get really married in the Church, couldn't I?"

"Do you have someone in mind?"

"You know David, don't you?"

"I see."

"We've kidded about it is all. But sometimes it seems the solution. I want so much to have children and Stanley has vetoed that."

Did she dream of a little line of Jamesons, all with enhanced smiles? Did he? It is a temptation for the celibate to find the amorous complications of the laity amusing, but, of course, they seldom really are. The statistics on unchurched marriages in the Archdiocese of Chicago were alarming. Not that sacramental marriages represented the solid rock they once had, but at least in them the vows made for some kind of check against folly. The Collinses were at a dangerous age—perhaps all ages are dangerous, but when forty comes and youth seems to be slipping away, there is an impulse to want to return to square one and begin all over again, as if life were a game that can be played and replayed over and over. But marriages can weaken when only one spouse wanders, and that puts the other in a tragic position. Still, Father Dowling had difficulty seeing Phyllis Collins as such a tragic figure.

One of them, Stanley or Phyllis, had come to him to get some kind of endorsement to dissolve their wobbly union, but which one was it?

"Perhaps if I talked with you and your husband together."

"He would never talk to a priest."

"But he has."

"What do you mean?"

"He was here on Monday."

"Stanley!"

"Yes."

Her eyes widened, more in fright than surprise. "What did he tell you?"

"You don't expect me to answer that. That is why it would be best if you both came together."

"He wouldn't listen to you."

"But you don't know what I would say."

She was confused. She no longer regarded him as an ally against outrageous fortune. "I think I can guess what he would have said."

"If you came together there would be no need of guessing."

For a half hour they hashed over what she had said, while Father Dowling considered that she provided him with a reason for believing her husband's accusations. Would she have invented her accusations against Stanley? He couldn't think so. The two of them had gotten themselves into a mess, a mess to which David Jameson had suggested a legalistic solution. A little learning is a dangerous thing indeed. Canon law assumed the theology of marriage, without which it was merely a set of rules. And David Jameson had obviously become an interested party as he dispensed his ill-digested lore to the weeping wife. What a solution he must have seemed to Phyllis. And to himself.

Finally she left, her tale having been told, if not with the upshot she must have expected. Father Dowling returned to his study and lit his pipe and reviewed the session with Phyllis Collins. There was a tap at the door and Marie Murkin looked in.

"I thought she had gone."

"As you see."

Marie waited expectantly, but she could not really think he would tell her about Phyllis's visit.

"She was certainly all dolled up."

"Was she?"

"Why don't people dress their age?"

"Have I ever complained?"

Marie stiffened. "About what?"

"Never mind."

"No, tell me."

"I was thinking of clerical clothes, Marie. The same in youth and middle age and afterward."

"Oh." She tugged her coat sweater about her.

"I like that sweater."

"This old thing?"

"There is something clerical about it."

"If you don't want to tell me, don't."

"But I just did."

After she left, he felt remorse. He had to curb his teasing of Marie. She was a good woman. At the moment her solid predictability seemed the rock on which civilization was raised.

Bob Oliver had come late to journalism, or vice versa. He had tried sales, even real estate after punishing months spent cramming for the licence exams, but all he had gained was a bad joke. "I specialize in houses and lots. Bawdy houses and lots of beer." Ho, ho. He didn't have the buddy-buddy gift of his brother-in-law, Stanley. Eventually, he had sense enough to get out of a line of work where he would always run a distant second to Stanley. One Realtor in a family is enough anyway. He went into food and found it boring. Finally, he parlayed his college English major into a job at the *Fox River Tribune*.

Not much of a job, but it sounded important. Even Stanley was impressed.

"Why don't you write a piece on Stanley?" Phyllis urged him.

"Too much like incest."

Incest was one thing Stanley wasn't guilty of, but only because he had no sister. Phyllis seemed totally unaware of her husband's reputation.

Bob did drop by the agency to see if there was any way he could write the story. The only one in the office when he got there was Susan Sawyer, and she responded to the possibility of a story on the agency with such enthusiasm that Bob never got around to telling her he was the brother of her husband's partner. Thought of that way, it seemed pretty remote anyway.

"Of course, you'd have to focus on George." She gave him a meaningful look. "Some partners are partners in name only."

He had taken that to be a remark on her marriage, and that made him more vulnerable to her charms than he might otherwise have been.

After she gave him a tour of the office, she put a hand on his arm. "This is not the place for an interview."

"What would you suggest?"

The bar at the Radisson, as it happened, adding to Bob's supposition that he was talking to a disenchanted spouse. Having a drink with her would probably be the end of the story anyway. He certainly didn't intend to write it to Susan Sawyer's specifications.

"You know an awful lot about the business," he said when they were settled at a table, out of the afternoon traffic of the bar.

"I'm an agent, too, you know."

"I did a little real estate myself for a time."

"And repented?" Again she put her hand on his arm.

"You have to do something bad in order to repent."

She found this funny. Bob in turn found her fascinating, in a middle-aged sort of way. A little stocky for his taste, but she had a way of leaning toward him when she spoke that suggested intimacy. The next time she put her hand on his arm he covered it with his own. That was the end of talk about real estate. Instead he got the story of her life. All the dreams of her girlhood seemed to have come to naught.

"Why does marriage have to be the end of everything?"

"Is it?"

"Aren't you married?"

"No."

"I find that hard to believe."

They were holding hands now, the ones that weren't on their drinks. Susan was drinking martinis and not holding them too well. The happy hour crowd was convening when they left. Her car was at the agency, and, outside, Bob talked her out of driving and offered to take her home. He saw her to the door and accepted her invitation to come in.

"I would say for a nightcap, but it's too early for that."

"Not unless you intend to take a nap."

Suddenly she was in his arms, her mouth pressed to his. The sequel was not something Bob cared to dwell on. She was voracious, and, when he finally left, he felt used. Susan was the kind of girl who would lead if you danced with her. One thing was definite, he was not going to write a story about the Sawyer-Collins agency. Not having told her that Phyllis was his sister seemed vaguely duplicitous, but all in all a plus. In the following weeks, she left several messages for him at the *Tribune,* but he ignored them. He should have enjoyed it when she complained about Stanley, but he didn't. She wasn't much easier on her husband, the man who had thwarted her youthful promise. Bob's abiding impression was, poor George Sawyer.

Bob did a feature on dentists instead, full of lore on orthodontics fed him by Dr. David Jameson, who seemed to mean it when he said that everyone has a natural right to a perfect smile. The dentist himself seemed pretty grim, but he was helpful, and Bob had cast him in the starring role. The story established Bob Oliver as the paper's human interest wiz. Once a week, he canonized some local figure, and hopeful subjects began to come to him. Most of them should have paid advertising rates for the boost Bob gave them. He always insisted on Sylvia Woods as his photographer. Her lens was as flattering as Bob's prose, and he began to think of her as Rosalind Russell to his Cary Grant in *His Girl Friday*, but there was no day in the week when she was his. None of his overtures introduced an operetta starring the two of them.

"Do all photographers have negative thoughts?"

"Only in the dark room."

"That's what I had in mind."

Her disdainful look would have turned a lesser man into a monk. What hurt was that she was susceptible to Stanley.

"He's your brother-in-law?" It was the first time Sylvia was really interested in anything he said. "You ought to do a piece on him."

"You sound like my sister."

"At most."

Disappointment did not dull his hopes. He told Sylvia what kind of husband Stanley was, but this seemed to pique her interest rather than the reverse. Were there any women nowadays like his sainted mother? She had been crushed when Phyllis got married in a civil ceremony, and until she died prayed a nonstop novena that her daughter would get her marriage blessed.

"It won't last," Bob assured her.

"I want it to last. But as a real marriage," his mother had said.

When Phyllis told him about the money Stanley was due to get when he turned fifty, Bob wanted the marriage to last, too. That would be compensation enough for Stanley's running around. What a crock that someone like Stanley was in line for an inheritance, even if he did have to wait for years until he got it.

Phyllis and their mother were more or less reconciled during Mrs. Oliver's last illness. Her dying wish was that her daughter should have her marriage blessed by the Church. Bob mentioned it to the Franciscan who came to give the last rites, expecting him to think of Phyllis's situation the way his mother did, but the friar just smiled indulgently.

"Will you talk to her, Father?"

"This may not be the best time."

Bob had thought of doing a story on permissive priests, but knocking people wasn't the style of his features.

At the paper, Bob shared an office with three other writers, but he had come to find the press room at the courthouse more congenial than the city room at the *Tribune*. It was more like an old movie set, hungover types hung over the keyboards of their computers, the air blue with cigarette smoke, an atmosphere of resentful and cynical discontent. It was one place where Bob Oliver felt unequivocally successful in his profession. The court reporters envied them. He found them fascinating company, feeling somewhat like Dante touring Purgatory. And Tuttle the lawyer was usually there, looking for an ambulance to chase. It turned out that Tuttle knew all about Stanley's inheritance.

"How come you know about it?"

"I looked it up."

"How much is it?"

"Lots."

"Real estate?"

Tuttle punched his arm. Maybe he didn't know how much

Stanley was due to get. Bob asked him how you looked up something like that, and he spent an afternoon with the lawyer going over the will of Frederick Collins. Well, it was hard to put an exact figure to an amount that was always growing larger. He tried to overcome his resentment by thinking that Phyllis would also benefit. In the meantime, she should do what she could about keeping her looks. He suggested she do something about her teeth.

"What do you mean?" But she half-covered her mouth with her hand when she spoke, as she usually did.

"Get them straightened. You have a natural right to a perfect smile."

He gave her a photocopy of his feature on dentists. "Tell Jameson you're my sister. He owes me."

The visit with Father Dowling had gone well, not that Stanley Collins was surprised; he had a gift with people. It was that, rather than ambition, that carried him as a Realtor, maybe not with the results his partner would have liked, but how could you sweat it out day after day when you knew that you were going to come into money no matter how unsuccessful the agency was? Besides, if anything happened, George would do all right. In the manner of partners, George Sawyer and Stanley Collins had taken out hefty insurance policies on one another, just in case. The premiums were paid by the agency, of course, but even so George grumbled that Stanley didn't carry his weight. Their arrangement was fifty-fifty, no matter the source of their profits, the lion's share of which were always due to George.

"Carrying my own weight is less of an effort in my case," Stanley said, poking a finger in his partner's huge belly like the witch in the fairy tale. "You ought to take better care of yourself, George."

Poor George was a sucker for every new diet that came along, and from time to time he actually lost some weight, but inevitably he would fall off his diet and balloon up again. Then he would resume his visits to the Rendezvous with Stanley, slopping up single malt scotch and gorging on cholesterol. It was George's crush on the singer there that got Stanley interested in her. Wanda Janski had a voice, no doubt of that, and in the dim lights of the bar, singing her heart out, she looked beautiful. The sentimental lyrics and the scotch made George forget his wife and yearn for the plush solace of Wanda. But when she joined them, it was clear to Stanley that it was himself she was interested in. At first Stanley's attentiveness to Wanda had been just an effort to annoy George, but the atmosphere of the Rendezvous worked its magic on him as well. When George mentioned their agency she said she was looking for a new apartment.

"Tell me what you'd like, and I'll find it," Stanley said, putting his hand on hers. Wanda drank only spritzers while she worked, just enough to keep a buzz on that did not interfere with her performance. "How many are there?"

"How many?" She looked at him.

"Husband, kids."

Her laugh seemed to draw on the human kindness of her ample breasts. "I'm single. In my work, I only meet guys like you."

"I wish I met gals like you in mine."

"So find me an apartment."

"I handle commercial property," George said despondently. "Apartments, houses, that's Stanley's side."

Stanley gave her a card, not really expecting to hear from her. Conversations in bars never really count.

"What a woman," George sighed when she left them.

"I think she likes you, George."

"Go to hell."

"You're just saying that because I'm worth so much to you dead."

"What a thing to say."

"It's true, isn't it?"

"I could say the same to you."

George turned his attention to Wanda, who had rejoined her accompanist at the piano. Later, when she sang "Danny Boy," George wept openly. Well, after all, he was married to Susan. Stanley was never bothered by thoughts of Phyllis on such occasions. Anyway, both their wives thought they were at a reunion in Milwaukee.

When Wanda called it took Stanley a minute before he remembered who she was. Shirley had been a little starchy when she said there was a woman on the phone. Young as she was, the office manager had the manner of a den mother and was always urging Stanley to carry his share of the business. She had come to suspect that when a woman called it was not a client.

"Have you found me an apartment?"

"Amazing that you should ask," Stanley said, playing for time. The voice was familiar, but he couldn't place it. "I was just about to call you."

She was free now, if he was.

"But I don't know where you live."

She told him.

"That's in your own name?"

Her laugh brought back memories of the singer at the Rendezvous. "Wanda, I'll be there before you can say Jack Robinson. Or sing 'Danny Boy.'"

When he got there, he couldn't see why she would want another apartment. But he looked the place over, professionally, and he noticed the plaited palm stuck behind a picture, a memento of Palm Sunday. In the kitchen was a religious calendar, St. Hilary's.

"I grew up there," he said.

"So did I."

In business, any hook on which you could hang a sale would do, but in minutes they were sipping Chablis and talking about the old parish. She had gone to the parish school, too.

"What year?"

She had been a couple years behind him. "My parents shipped me off to military school."

Why did that always interest women? Somehow it did. Stanley told her all about it, and went on to the years at Marquette.

"I see you're married."

Stanley never took off his wedding band. It was a superstition. He felt that if he took off the ring, the legal paper that bound him to Phyllis would shrivel, grow yellow, dissolve into dust.

"Not in the Church."

"Oh."

"A civil ceremony."

"Any kids?"

"No."

Why did his life suddenly seem a string of empty events, the stupid military school, Marquette, his partnership with George Sawyer? Even Wanda seemed to find it sad, no matter the interest she showed. He almost told her he would inherit a bundle when he was fifty. He did tell her, later, when his visits became a ritual, weekly at least.

"This is good wine."

"It's from the supermarket."

"Actually I don't like white wine."

"So I'll buy some red." Already it was clear this wasn't a chat between a Realtor and a client.

"There were Collinses who lived on Lincoln Avenue."

"That was us."

"Funny we never knew one another."

"Well, now we do."

"Now we do."

"Wanda, there's nothing wrong with this apartment."

"Who said there was?"

"So why are you looking for another?"

"Do you always believe what you're told?"

In the bedroom, there was a print of a Renaissance Madonna on the wall, and behind it more palm.

"You still go to Mass?" With the drapes pulled and the mild glow of wine, afterward they would lie in her bed for hours and talk about anything.

"Not as much as I should."

"I don't go at all."

Maybe it was the fact that they had both grown up in St. Hilary's, but religion became a frequent topic. And after Phyllis had told him what she had learned about Church law, Stanley naturally talked it over with Wanda.

"If that's true, I'm as much married to you as I am to Phyllis."

"If it's possible for her, it's possible for you."

"What do you mean?"

"Now what could I possibly mean?"

Stanley knew a sudden panic. One thing about a wedding band, it prevented things going beyond a roll in the hay, no matter how frequent. He liked Wanda, he really did, and he had become used to their afternoons together. When he listened to her sing at the club it was not just imagination that she was directing all those steamy ballads to him. When George Sawyer fell off his most recent diet and came along, he noticed that Wanda treated Stanley like a lover. Stanley denied it in a way that made it clear it was a gentleman's denial.

"You could go to Mass again," Wanda said.

He had told her, half sincerely, that he missed the religion that he had lost, but his marriage had cut him off from it.

"You could receive Communion."

She might as well have been proposing to him. Let Phyllis marry that bastard Jameson, and he and Wanda could stand before the altar at St. Hilary's while Father Dowling said the nuptial Mass.

He sat up on the edge of the bed, anxious to get out of there. It was one thing to be enraged by what Phyllis had said, to feel that his wife was betraying him, but he sure as hell wasn't going to pull such a stunt himself. Not with Wanda, not with anybody.

"Wanda, I am as married as I'll ever be."

"Even if she leaves you?"

"She won't."

They were both out of bed now, and Wanda pulled on her colorful muumuu. Stanley was getting dressed. By the time he was in the living room, he had made up his mind.

"I am going to stop giving her any reason to leave me."

"And I'm the reason."

"I told you what she said."

"Get out of here."

"Now, Wanda . . ."

"Go, you sonofabitch. I mean it. I'll be damned if I'll provide your wife with a reason to leave you. Stay with her. You deserve one another."

"Wanda, you don't understand. Sure, I'll *tell* her I'm not seeing you anymore, but . . ."

She missed him when she threw the wineglass, and he was outside pulling the door closed when the heavy ashtray hit it. He hurried down to his car.

David Jameson's father had been a barber with a four-chair shop at a time when men got their hair cut once a week. The helpers he hired came and went, there was always a plentiful supply, and business was good. First, there was his location, on Dirksen and Fourth, right in the heart of the business district. A man could make an appointment, get his hair cut, and be back at his desk in half an hour. Jameson Sr.'s hair was thin, and he slicked it back on his head with witch hazel. David had his mother's hair but his dental office was not unlike his father's shop.

He had two assistants, young men who were paying off their student loans and had not yet opened their own offices, a species of apprentice, and older dentists who wanted to keep their hands in part-time. There were seven dental chairs, three of which were David's. He scheduled patients in bunches and was able to attend to three simultaneously, thanks to a very efficient dental nurse and a succession of technologists who were trained to do the preliminary work and to wind it up afterward. He used up a dozen pairs of latex gloves an hour, flitting back and forth, but he himself bade each patient good-bye and he prided himself on the belief that none of them thought of his office as an assembly line.

When Bob Oliver had approached him about doing a feature on dentists, David had snatched the opportunity. He made himself available, he devoted a great deal of time to providing the reporter with information, he figured in all the photographs eventually used. Not all had been used, but he bought them all from the *Tribune*, had them framed and hung them about the office. A handsome reprint of the original article was available in his waiting room.

"How many patients do you handle at the same time?" Oliver had asked.

"I can only work on one patient at a time," he answered carefully.

That had been the only dangerous moment, but then Oliver was not the kind of writer who sought to balance praise with blame. The feature had been a tremendous boon. Not least because Oliver sent his sister Phyllis for a consultation.

Phyllis was the kind of woman his parents would not have liked. David was surprised that he himself found her attractive. It is not easy for a woman in a dental chair to retain desirability. Sometimes David thought all those open mouths had kept him single. Phyllis was somehow different, fearful of pain, childlike, yet completely trusting.

"Where are the pictures of your family?" Phyllis asked when their sessions got under way. From the outset, he had scheduled her alone for an hour, not wishing to entrust her to any latex-gloved hands but his own. She was a small woman, but for all that every bit a woman, as she had made little effort to conceal. Bridget, the nurse, had ventured to say something disparaging about the way Mrs. Collins dressed, but she had never made that mistake again.

"My parents are dead."

"I meant your own family."

"I have none."

"You're not married?"

"Who would have me?" he asked, surprising himself.

"Oh, you."

He turned down the Muzak when she was in the chair, not wanting to miss a word she managed to say while he was working on her smile. She enjoyed returning to the fact that he was unmarried, and he found he liked discussing it with her.

"It is such a serious step."

"Are you Catholic?" she asked.

"Yes, I am."

"I was raised Catholic."

"What happened?" Is this why she had been brought to him, that he might give her wise counsel, perhaps lead her back to the faith? She told him of her marriage, and soon that became their great topic. He suggested that it was something they might discuss in less trying surroundings, thinking of the ever-watchful Bridget.

They had lunch together, on a Wednesday when there was no need to hurry, and she was fascinated when he spoke to her of the canon law of marriage.

"How do you know all these things?"

"I once thought I would become a priest."

"You would have made a wonderful priest."

He patted her hand and felt devoured by the smile that was now almost perfect. She turned her hand over and held his. That was when she told him about her husband.

"I can't tell you what that does to a woman." She meant the discovery that her husband was unfaithful.

"It must be a terrible cross."

"I don't think I could ever do that."

"I should hope not." He felt the pressure of her hand.

Too soon her smile was all that it had been intended by nature to be, but he was reluctant to let it end. There was still so much he had to say to this troubled soul. An annual checkup would be as bad as a final good-bye. He carefully examined her mouth and said he wanted her to make another appointment.

"I do root canals, you know."

"Oh my God."

He smiled. Once the procedure had rightly struck terror in patients, but there was no longer need for that. She agreed to X-rays, and when she returned she wept in his chair as they talked. It was all he could do not to gather her in his arms. Only with reluctance did he tell her a root canal was unnecessary.

When Bob Oliver hailed him on the street, David Jameson turned and felt the leap of guilt. Was this an irate brother come to avenge his sister's honor? Of course, nothing had happened as yet, but David no longer thought that his heart was pure with respect to Phyllis. But Oliver was so affable it was a relief.

"I don't suppose dentists drink."

"Only in moderation." How playful he suddenly felt, thinking, this is her brother.

They had a drink in the bar of the Calumet Hotel, sitting at an out-of-the-way table. Oliver congratulated Jameson on his sister's new smile. "The man who brings a smile to women's mouths" had been one of the less happy phrases in Oliver's feature article.

"I think she is pleased with the result."

"I wish everything was as pleasant for her."

And then, unbidden, not unwelcome, came Bob's version of the story of Phyllis's marital problems, but Oliver's was not a theological approach.

"If he wasn't going to inherit a fortune, I'd tell her to leave him."

"A fortune?"

And so David had learned the story of the great event that would happen on Stanley Collins's fiftieth birthday.

"How old is he now?"

"Forty-four."

"That's not too long to wait," David said carefully.

"But what if he doesn't?"

"What do you mean?"

"What if he should dump her?"

"Divorce her?"

It was not a wholly unpleasant thought, looked at from a non-theological point of view. Or even from one. In the eyes of the Church, Phyllis was not truly married to Stanley Collins.

"Maybe that would be best."

"After she has stuck with him through hell and high water, best to be cut off from the money that's coming to him?"

"I hadn't thought of it that way."

"Collins better not think of any way, I can tell you that."

Oliver had become surly with drink, but that was a small price to pay for these confidences.

Bridget Carroll had received only two glancing mentions in the article that had appeared in the *Tribune*, but in half the photographs she was at Dr. Jameson's side, assisting as he worked on a patient. Sylvia, the photographer, had made sure that the face of the patient was not shown, but it was her insistence that put Bridget in so many of the shots. A little feminine solidarity, Bridget supposed, not that she had discontents along those lines. It was the fact that David was single that added zest to her job, and she rightly felt that she had become indispensable to him. Dentists came and went, the young ones, and those who were retired handled patients they had acquired in their own practice when they came to work for David and were perfectly content not to take on new ones.

When the article appeared, Bridget had bought half a dozen copies of that issue of the paper. It was at her suggestion that the story had become a brochure that was available in the waiting room. And it was Bridget who had called Sylvia Woods to see about buying the whole set of the photographs she had taken, had them framed, and decorated the office walls with them. Laura, who handled appointments and payments and answered the phone, had been immortalized at her several tasks, but none of those photographs had appeared in the *Tribune,* so she was especially happy to have the framed ones hung about. There was an immediate influx of new patients as a result of the article, but, of course, there was Mrs. Collins, too. In the informal manner of dental offices, she became just Phyllis.

Men are fools, of course, particularly where women like Phyllis Collins are concerned, but it came as a shock that David was susceptible to her pathetic efforts to be girlish. However, Bridget's allusion to the shortness of Phyllis's skirt brought a rebuke from David.

"I could put a blanket over her lap."

"What do you mean?"

"This place is like thigh land when she's in the chair."

He bristled. "That's enough of that, Bridget. I mean it."

Stunned, Bridget had gone away on her crepe soles for a remorseful cigarette in the ladies. She kept a bottle of mouthwash there to remove the scent of cigarette smoke from her breath. As she swished and gargled, she looked at herself in the mirror. She was thirty-five, an age that seemed to have just crept up on her, but she had the look of a colleen: jet black hair, pale skin, a dusting of freckles, and great round blue eyes. And her smile was her own. David often had her smile for a patient to show what effect he was striving for. That meant he noticed her, but it seemed only a professional notice, as if she were an advertisement for his skills. Her reflected eyes flashed with anger at the memory of being scolded by David.

That had been only the beginning. David preferred to work alone when Phyllis Collins was in the chair and since she was the only appointment for the hour, Bridget had what should have been a welcome break.

"Is Mini Haha in the chair?" Laura asked.

"Mrs. Collins?"

She had half a mind to scold Laura as David had her, but she couldn't have been convincing. "With legs like those you'd think she'd wear slacks."

If Bridget did not scold, neither could she enter into Laura's catty appraisal. It would have sounded like sour grapes. She took comfort in the fact that eventually Phyllis Collins would have the smile nature intended her to have, and that would be the end of that.

But when the orthodontist had performed his wonders, he scheduled another appointment for Phyllis, and even though Bridget had examined the X-rays, she feared he would perform an unnecessary root canal just to keep her in the chair. But that wasn't the end of it.

He phoned Phyllis from the office regularly, and Bridget became convinced he was seeing that woman Wednesdays when the office was closed. The address of the Collinses was in Phyllis's files and one Wednesday, trying to tell herself it was just an accidental turn, she drove past the address, and there was David's Chrysler at the curb. She went past the house in the other direction, too, wondering what was going on inside. She could have wept with frustration.

It wasn't simply that, however unconsciously, she had for the past four years gone to work in the hope that something would somehow happen between herself and David, there was also anger that he should be drawn to such a tart as Phyllis. And married at that.

That was the biggest surprise, in a way, given the thing David made of his religion. Before Phyllis, when he and Bridget would relax and chat after the last patient of the day, David had told her of his youthful desire to be a priest.

"I can believe it."

He was pleased. "Why do you say that?"

"Well, you haven't married."

"Is that what the priesthood means to you—celibacy?" He still wore the pleased expression.

"I was never drawn to it."

He frowned. "Women will never be ordained."

"That's all right with me."

He seemed reassured. Good Lord. But it underscored his own seriousness as a Catholic. Bridget had thought that might be what finally brought them together, her and David. She began to attend Mass at St. Hilary's after David had spoken of the pastor with high praise. David went to the ten o'clock on Sundays, so that became Bridget's habit as well. He always sat near the front, and he was conspicuous because of his height as well as because of the obvious devotion with which he followed the Mass. That he was still there every Sunday even after Phyllis Collins became a patient gave Bridget hope. He couldn't be up to anything with her and then go to Communion.

It was attendance at St. Hilary's that got Bridget involved with Edna Hospers and the senior center. That is where Bridget came to spend her Wednesday afternoons. She and Edna were soon good friends. They would have coffee together in Edna's office where it was okay if Bridget wanted a cigarette.

"Go ahead. My Earl smokes, and of course Father Dowling often has a pipe here."

Bridget steered clear of Marie Murkin, not an easy thing to do since the housekeeper seemed to watch for her. And then she was snared one Sunday morning.

"Is it true you work for Dr. Jameson?"

Bridget assumed Marie must have seen the story in the paper, but Marie said, "Edna mentioned it."

Bridget admitted that she worked for David. She already knew he was a great friend of the pastor's, but Marie seemed to have a different attitude toward him.

"A spoiled priest," Marie said, exposing her denture in a smile.

"A what?"

"That's what a man who wanted to be one but didn't is called."

"I didn't know that."

"That he wanted to be a priest?"

Bridget did not want to be quizzed about her employer, and she managed to escape. With Edna she could talk about David, girl to girl, so to speak.

"Do you see him aside from the office?" Edna asked.

"I wish."

"Ah."

After that, it was understood between them that she had a thing for David Jameson. Edna even talked of arranging something, asking Bridget and David for dinner, but Bridget vetoed it. At least for now. It would have seemed contrived.

"It would be. That's the idea."

Oh, dear God, it was good to be able to talk about it, not that it really helped all that much. Oh, yes it did. It helped some anyway. And then Edna learned about David and Phyllis Collins.

"Marie told me, so, of course, it's probably not true."

"It's true." And Bridget burst into tears.

"But she's married."

"And he's a man."

Sometimes Willie Boiardo thought he hated music, his fingers feeling along the keys of the piano as he thought the thought. All those lessons when he was a kid, the inevitable ambition under the praise of one teacher after another, the fellowship at Juilliard, and then suddenly he was on the job market. He could play the whole repertoire of Mozart's sonatas effortlessly from memory, but in the meantime he took a job as pianist in an orchestra that toured the provinces, playing at proms when kids still danced like human beings. All that collapsed in the late sixties, with everything else, and by then any thought of a career as a concert pianist had floated away on clouds of grass and coke. His agent found him work playing in bars for drunks and illicit couples. Nonetheless, at the piano, Willie gave it all he had. Finally, Wanda had heard him and their agents arranged a deal and he became the invisible partner in her performance.

"Music" was popular music to Wanda. She sang from memory rather than by reading the notes, and when they practiced it was a joy to develop the right arrangement for her. When he had it, she knew, and that was that. No need to explain to her the technicalities, which she wouldn't have understood anyway. Wanda was in her early thirties when they teamed up; she might have been his daughter, but Willie made love to her on his keyboard while she entranced the clientele with her voice. He was invisible to the listeners, there at the piano, and he was invisible to Wanda as well. As often as not, she forgot to ask for a hand for her accompanist, and when she did, Willie had no illusions that his artistry was appreciated. He didn't care. Wanda sang to the world at large, but Willie played only for her.

On breaks, Willie went to the bar where he drank in anonymity. It was enough that Joe Perzel, the bartender, recognized who he was and put the tumbler of bourbon before him, one of the perks of playing. Wanda just disappeared. After they got booked into the Rendezvous, after they became a permanent fixture there, she got a dressing room where she could rest between sets.

Everyone fell in love with her; that went without saying. For women, she was the torch singer they had dreamt of being, for men she was the woman of her songs, tragically in love, filled with longing, pleading for their response. Willie understood this. It was his own reaction to her singing. Wanda was an earth mother, eager to take you in her embrace. At least while she sang. It seemed to have no carryover once the lights went up, the applause swelled, and she was off to her dressing room. She might have been a nun, so far as Willie could see.

They practiced twice a week, at the Frosinone Hotel where he lived, not wanting to go stale, polishing up the songs that worked, adding others from time to time. Those morning sessions, when only his hands seemed sober, were golden times for Willie. He and Wanda were a team.

"Willie, without you I would be nothing."

"You could sing a cappella and hold the room."

"Before we got together I was on my way to being a has-been."

"Hey, you're talking to one."

"You're so damned good, Willie. How did you end up like this?"

"Good luck."

She kissed him on the forehead. He could have been a customer. If he had the gift of gab, he would have told her that he would rather play for her than give a concert in Carnegie Hall. That had once seemed a possibility, but to hell with it. He wouldn't trade playing to a paid audience in evening clothes for sitting in the smoky dark, backing up Wanda as she took her listeners by the heart and gave at least a passing meaning to the basic sadness of life.

"Is it the junk, Willie? You could kick it."

"Easily," he lied. "Growing up consists of outliving the dreams of youth."

"Who said that?"

"Aren't we alone?"

Another kiss on the forehead.

He did get off the hard stuff, settling for grass, half expecting her to notice and applaud. But he, like his piano, was an instrument, a means, background. Wanda was the star and Willie gloried in her borrowed light. And then along came Stanley Collins.

If he had designed the kind of bastard he hoped Wanda would avoid, he couldn't have come closer than Stanley Collins. At first he didn't believe Wanda could take such a small-town hotshot seriously, even if this was her small town. She began to take her breaks in a booth with Stanley. From the bar Willie had observed the progress of the relationship with disbelief and dread. Finally he made the mistake of telling Wanda what he thought of Stanley.

"It would take three of him to make a man, Wanda. Don't encourage him."

"Hey, do I try to run your life?"

"I'm not trying to run your life. I'm speaking as a friend."

"Okay, you've spoken."

In vain. What Wanda and Stanley had in common was their childhood in Fox River. And they both were Catholics.

"I didn't know you were Catholic, Wanda."

"Half the world is Catholic."

"I'm not."

"What are you?"

"Presbyterian!" It just came out. Willie hadn't been to church in half a century.

"Get together with another Presbyterian and you'll understand."

Willie asked around about Stanley, discreetly, and it was worse than he would have thought. The guy was a total ass, a suit, zilch. But Wanda was a woman, and, increasingly, Stanley was her man. When he was in the room, she sang to him. And she was seeing him during the day.

Wanda had rented an apartment when the deal with the Rendezvous became permanent, but Willie distrusted security and kept his room at the Frosinone. It was a hotel on the skids, his kind of place, he became part of the background there, the permanent guest no one noticed. He had an old upright in his room on which he played Mozart, using a lot of soft pedal so the rapping on the walls wouldn't begin. Someone rented a room for the night and thought they owned the hotel.

Willie was not proud of his spying, but he had to know how

serious Wanda was about Stanley. As for Stanley, nothing Willie had learned suggested he could be serious about anyone but Stanley. At least once a week they spent the afternoon together in Wanda's apartment. Willie got so he could recognize the car and know Stanley was up there. The affair was a threat to what he realized he considered his life. What the hell would happen to him if Wanda ever decided to break up their partnership? Stanley Collins was a menace, there was no doubt about it.

"You should get married and settle down, Wanda."

"You trying to get rid of me?"

"This is no life for a woman."

"No sale, Willie. You're stuck with me."

If she had admitted it, he might have doubted her. He became convinced that Stanley Collins was going to put him on the dust-heap of has-beens. The thought filled him with terror.

The Frosinone Hotel had been the U. S. Grant until the Pianone family took it over and renamed it after their ancestral city. Architecturally, it claimed to have been designed by someone in the Sullivan school, and it was this claim that Bob Oliver had come to inquire about when he was considering an article about the buildings of Fox River.

The way the reporter looked around the lobby made Primo Verdi, the manager, certain the Frosinone would not make the cut. Verdi led him to an arrangement of chairs in a corner of the lobby and, as luck would have it, Oliver got the chair with the broken leg. He tipped to one side as he settled in.

"Here, take this one," Verdi urged.

Oliver made a gesture with his hand. "I feel tilted anyway. Why hasn't this place been condemned?"

"For what?"

"For impersonating a hotel."

Oliver put his notebook back in a side pocket, leaning to do so, a movement which made him more or less upright, given the tilt of his chair. "Seriously, I thought this place was closed."

"We're open twenty-four hours a day."

Verdi wasn't worried about this visit. One, he could see the Frosinone would not figure in any article Bob Oliver wrote about the city's architecture. Two, nothing got into the papers the Pianones did not want to get in, so why worry? He satisfied the reporter's curiosity about the rundown hotel that it was Verdi's fate to manage.

Fifty percent occupancy isn't too bad for any hotel, and the Frosinone could count on that. Two floors, six and seven, were assigned to the model escorts who brought their johns to the Frosinone, and then there were the permanent residents, those who rented by the month, guests like Willie Boiardo, the musician. When his neighbors complained about Willie's piano, Verdi would ask him to play on the grand in the ballroom, the piano Willie used when he practiced with Wanda, his partner. Verdi was an audience of one as Willie went through a repertoire of operatic themes. What was an artist like Willie doing playing in a joint, Verdi wanted to know.

"Speaking of which," Willie said.

"I left it in your room, in the bathroom cabinet."

Maybe that was the difference, concert pianists didn't get hooked on drugs. Willie's supply was courtesy of the Pianones, the message enigmatically delivered by Peanuts, the Pianone nephew who was impersonating a cop.

"You try to collect, I'll break your legs."

One of the uncles, the head of the family, had heard Willie play on the ballroom grand, and when he learned of the musician's habit, offered to finance a cure.

"Who's sick?"

The uncle had shrugged. The role of reformer didn't fit him. But he resolved to take care of Willie's habit gratis. Hence the message from Peanuts.

Tuttle, the lawyer, usually accompanied Peanuts on his periodic visits, which were no doubt meant to make sure Verdi was not taking money from Willie Boiardo.

"I like this place," Tuttle would say, pushing his tweed hat to the back of his head and looking around the lobby. "It's got class."

Tuttle also professed to like the food in the hotel restaurant where the chandeliers and elegant china were mementos of the great days of the hotel. The same menu was now offered every day of the week, but Tuttle always pored over it as if it represented a new challenge. Verdi joined their table from time to time, having a glass of wine while Tuttle and Peanuts enjoyed their Salisbury steaks. These two were beer drinkers and complained when bottles were not brought to the table. Verdi told the waiter to put the beer in a wine bucket. He had a residual sense of what was fitting in the former U. S. Grant hotel.

"How's business, Tuttle?"

"Good, good." He chewed reflectively. "I don't think I've ever had Salisbury steak like this."

"Many people say that." But not with the admiration there was in Tuttle's voice.

"I told Bob Oliver about this place. He's thinking of doing one of his features on Fox River hotels."

"He came by."

"Was his photographer with him?" Tuttle asked slyly.

"I don't think he was impressed by the Frosinone."

"Good," Peanuts said.

All in all, a conversation with these two was about as rewarding as one with Boiardo. Many jobs are boring, but working in a hotel carries boredom to new depths. Verdi stayed because leaving would involve a decision, and he had quit making decisions. He was sixty years old and what future he had stretched before him like a barren moonscape. There had been a time when the sight of one of the model escorts would awaken an earlier version of himself, but Verdi tried to tell himself that all that was behind him now. He would have had no regrets if it were. In his experience, women were poison, and the consolations did not begin to make up for the aggravation. He had married three times and none of them had lasted a year. The last wife he had brought to his suite in the hotel, and within a week she was crawling the walls.

"There's nothing to do!" Her name was Flora and he had met her on a plane coming back from a weekend in Vegas. They lined up the empty little liquor bottles on their trays as they winged their way back to Chicago. When they landed, they headed for a bar in O'Hare. Verdi decided he was in love just before he passed out in the O'Hare Hilton. When he awoke with a roaring head and the roar of ascending and descending planes all around him, he was surprised to find Flora beside him. She opened her puffy eyes.

"You said we'd get married."

So they got married, and he brought her back to the Frosinone where she learned the meaning of boredom. Then, one day in the lobby, one of the girls from the sixth floor cried out, "Flora! Where have you been?"

"Vegas."

"I thought you was in Pittsburgh."

Obviously they had worked together. That was the end of Flora so far as Verdi was concerned, and he didn't nix her plan to move onto the sixth floor and go back to work. He asked Tuttle to handle the divorce but the tweed hat went north and south. "I don't take divorce cases."

"Don't you have to?"

"I'd turn in my licence first."

"Geez. What's the big deal?"

"Marriage is sacred."

"You married?"

"No."

"I thought so. I could tell you stories."

Mrs. Stanley Collins would be included in future stories. That night she showed up as the shy partner in a dubious couple. The guy she was with signed in as Jones and paid cash in advance. A real quickie, they were gone in an hour. Verdi looked forward to telling Bob Oliver the story, knowing the lady was his sister, running the risk of being hit by the reporter. Well, he would enjoy it in anticipation. Oliver would have trouble getting out of the broken chair in the lobby, giving Verdi time to flee to the safety of the desk. In his anticipating mind's eye Oliver just glared at him and then went through the revolving doors. Or tried to. They were on the fritz. He was lucky he hadn't been caught in them. He got out of the revolving doors and out of the hotel and Verdi breathed an imagined sigh of relief.

Phil Keegan, captain of detectives in the Fox River police department, parked on the road that ran along the side of St. Hilary's rectory and went across the lawn to the kitchen door. He entered without knocking, and Marie turned from the stove and looked at him without surprise.

"Were you at the noon Mass?"

"Couldn't make it. Does he have a guest for lunch?"

"If you stay."

"Good."

He wanted to make sure that Jameson, the dentist, wasn't hanging around. The man had become a frequent presence and Phil realized he resented it. The fact was he was a little jealous. He considered himself Roger Dowling's closest friend, at least among lay people, and the rectory had become a haven for him. Long ago Phil had been at Quigley, a couple classes behind Roger Dowling, but Latin had proved too much for him, and at that time Latin was crucial for anyone thinking of the priesthood. So Phil had left and eventually married and became a cop. When his wife died, the bottom fell out of his life. His two daughters were married, and each lived hundreds of miles away. A life of loneliness loomed. Then Roger Dowling had been made pastor of St. Hilary's. Phil told Roger he had known him at Quigley, one thing led to another, and soon Phil was a welcome guest at the rectory without need of an invitation.

Roger liked to hear of the cases they were working on, and often his priestly interest was engaged. If Phil was the representative of justice, Roger represented mercy, and their friendship was proof that the two were compatible. The smarmy Jameson seemed to jeopardize that.

"It's not Wednesday," Marie said.

"Who said it was?"

"Wednesday is the dentist's day off."

He should have known Marie would notice what he thought of Jameson. He suspected she thought pretty much the same thing herself. Roger was another story. The pastor might tease Marie, and Phil, too, if he had a chance, but Phil had never heard him knock another person. He realized he would have been shocked if Roger revealed a distaste for Jameson, or anyone else. It brought home to him how much of ordinary conversation consists in raking others over the coals. Roger was critical of the Cubs, of course, but that was necessary for salvation, or at least for peace of mind.

Several times Roger had jokingly referred to himself as a penitent and maybe that was the basis for his acceptance of others. Phil knew what he had meant. The pressures of the marriage tribunal had driven Roger gradually to drink. Eventually that had spelled the end of what until then had been a promising clerical career. Roger went off for a cure in Wisconsin, but the real cure had been St. Hilary's. This was the life he had wanted to lead as a priest, a pastor, not a bureaucrat sitting in a downtown office processing hopeless pleas for annulment.

Phil was sitting at the kitchen table having what Roger would have referred to as a preprandial beer when the pastor came in. His face lit up at the sight of Phil.

"Just a homeless person looking for a handout, Roger."

"Welcome to the soup kitchen."

"Soup kitchen!" Marie cried. "Well, I like that."

"What's on?" Phil asked, looking toward the stove. "It smells good."

Marie shooed them into the dining room where Roger said grace slowly in Latin and then, on signal, Marie came in with lunch.

"Eggs benedict!" Phil said. "I love them."

"Blesséd eggs," Roger murmured. "Or blessed eggs. Or maybe monastic."

Phil ignored him. There were moments with Roger when it was necessary to ignore obscure remarks. No doubt they made sense in some world or other. This one seemed to rely on Latin, so Phil was doubly shy.

"I didn't see you at Mass."

"I wasn't there."

"Busy?"

Phil nodded, concentrating on the food. Marie had brought him another beer, pouring it for him with great deference. In the kitchen he could drink from the bottle, but not in the dining room. There was always beer, and harder stuff in the rectory, as if Roger were still proving to himself that it held no attraction for him.

Marie came and went and finally sat at the end of the table closest to the kitchen, side saddle, ready to jump up if need be.

"Busy with what?"

"A hit-and-run. Cy went to the morgue with the body."

Marie made a face. "No details, please."

"I don't have any."

"Who was killed?"

Phil chewed thoughtfully and took a drink of beer. "He was a Realtor. Nobody you would know."

"A Realtor?"

"A partner in the Sawyer and Collins Agency."

A moment's silence, and then Marie asked, "Which one?"

Phil realized that Father Dowling was looking at him intently. Marie, too, was staring.

"Collins."

"My God."

❧ Part Two ❧

The Fox River police department had neither the personnel nor the bureaucratic division of labor of its big city counterparts, but even in its modest compartmentalization, hit-and-runs fell within the scope of the detective division's purview. Thus, if he were capable of expressing surprise, Cy Horvath might have reacted to Phil Keegan's interest in the death of Stanley Collins.

"Friend of yours?"

"Father Dowling knew him."

"Ah."

Phil's expression changed, the look of a man who had not been made privy to what the pastor of St. Hilary's knew of the dead man.

"I'll look into it," Cy said.

"Good idea. At least have someone do it."

"Someone" in this instance turned out to be Agnes Lamb. She was capable of showing surprise and proved it.

"A hit-and-run?"

"So far as we know."

Her eyes widened and she nodded. "I'll look into it."

It turned out that no one else had. Traffic was on an Italian strike. One of the meter maids had Chief Robertson's wife's SUV ticketed and towed. It had been a clear violation—two hours in a one-hour handicap place—but Mrs. Robertson had come to think that the law did not apply to the wife of the chief of police. Robertson had preferred to take on the Traffic division rather than his wife, and the result had been an unannounced slow-down. It had been a week since a traffic ticket had been issued. The officer who held out the longest was promised the Gracie Robertson Prize, a blowup photograph of the chief on which target rings had been superimposed. A set of darts was included. Agnes's courtesy call at Traffic was meant to forestall any complaint of encroachment. In the event she was given carte blanche.

"What do you have on the accident?"

"Nothing."

So she started with the newspaper report.

The body had been found on Bailey Street, which ran parallel to Dirksen Boulevard, a major downtown street, but Bailey was all but unknown except to the patrons of the Rendezvous Club, one of the places of business that had transformed the street from the residential haven it once was. The reporter had found that Collins was well known at the Rendezvous and had been there the previous evening. What condition had he been in when he stepped into the night from the club?

"Condition?"

"Had he been drinking?"

"This is a bar."

"Was he drunk?"

No answer. The inquiry conjured up the picture of a man reeling out of the Rendezvous and heading up the street on foot toward the parking lot. He would have been all but invisible to approaching vehicles.

"Was his car in the club parking lot?" Cy asked when Agnes told him this.

"Yup."

"So he never got to it."

"Maybe it got to him."

When Agnes explained, Cy returned to the parking lot with her.

The lot occupied a place where a building had been removed, like a tooth extracted from the row of once residential houses now converted to office space for a variety of small businesses. Agnes was driving and she pulled into the lot. At this time of day it was all but deserted. The car they had come to see was parked in the center of the lot, at an angle. It had the look of having been parked hastily and then left. Had Stanley Collins been that anxious for a drink? And then Cy noticed the fender.

It was the far side of the car, the left fender. There were streaks of blood on the hood. Cy circled the car in silence. The sturdier sort of weed lined the edges of the lot and, in the afternoon sun, filled the air with sweetness of a sort.

"What do you think?" Agnes said.

"Looks like it hit something."

"You mean someone."

Cy nodded. Agnes was waiting for him to say it. Had Stanley Collins been run over by his own car?

"Well?" Agnes said.

"I don't think this one was an accident."

"I'll have the car taken downtown."

"We can wait for them to get here."

In the meantime, Cy circled the car again. It seemed best not to touch anything. The car had tinted glass, but the windshield permitted a look at the front seat.

"What's that?" Cy asked Agnes. He stepped aside so she could take a better look.

"A scarf?"

"Maybe."

It took half an hour for the tow truck from the police garage to show up. The driver wore a greasy baseball cap, Ben Franklin glasses, and a tee shirt that stretched over his enormous belly.

"Whose car is it, Mrs. Robertson's?"

His smile revealed a gap between his upper teeth. He turned and released a spray of tobacco juice. His assistant, a college kid hired for the summer, danced out of range. The two did not inspire confidence.

"Maybe we should have the lab send a crew here, Agnes."

The driver took umbrage at this. "Even if I touch the damned thing my prints are on record."

"What were you in for?"

"Oh, come on."

Even so, Cy stayed close as they hooked up the car and then pulled it onto the flatbed truck.

"My fingerprints are on the car," Agnes said to Cy when they had stepped away.

The car had been unlocked when she found it and the registration had told her it belonged to the deceased Stanley Collins.

"That's how I know it's a scarf on the front seat."

Before they left, Cy went over to check out those sweet-smelling weeds. Who decides if something is a weed and not a flower?

"Why did you ask if it was Mrs. Robertson's car?" Agnes was asking the driver when he came back.

"It's a long story."

Cy told Agnes the story on the drive downtown, following the flatbed with Stanley Collins's car aboard.

"I thought they were a little funny in Traffic."

"They always are."

He had Agnes drop him at the morgue.

At the morgue Cy tried not to notice how beautiful Dr. Pippin, the assistant coroner, was. Would he have stayed if Lubins were performing the autopsy? Pippin's lab coat hung to her knees but could not conceal her graceful body. Her tawny pony tail tossed as she went about her grisly task, talking into the microphone suspended above her. Why would someone go through medical school and then settle for a job as assistant coroner? It was one of those mysteries that fascinated Cy about Pippin. Of course, he was waiting for her to finish so they could talk. She represented an occasion of sin of sorts, not that he would ever say or do anything, but there are sins of thought and Cy fought against them manfully. He loved his wife, and Pippin now had a husband, a double protection against anything stupid on his part. On her part, there was only a cheery friendliness. She might have been his sister.

"Poor devil," she said, when she emerged. "Hungry?"

"Are you?"

"Famished."

"I'll buy you lunch."

"You will not. It's my turn."

They went across the street to the sports bar, another precaution. It was filled with cops and reporters, and no one would wonder what he was doing having lunch with Pippin. Her own attitude was so devoid of anything romantic that Cy had only to mimic it. She ordered a Reuben and a beer, and Cy had the goulash.

"Is it Hungarian?"

He put his ear near the plate. "Can't tell. What killed him?"

"A car."

She chewed her sandwich and smiled at the same time. Very distracting, but Cy was a Hungarian whose face betrayed nothing. In fact he had only one expression. Well, maybe one and a half. He was wearing the half.

"Dead on the scene?"

"He whacked his head on the curb. The car drove across his rib cage. It would have been quick."

"It was reported at six-thirty."

"He probably lay there for hours."

"How many?"

She shrugged, chewed, looked at the ceiling. "Four, five."

"Early morning?"

"Probably. After midnight."

"His name was Stanley Collins."

"Did you know him?"

"He was a Realtor. He sold me my house."

She put down her sandwich. "Tell me about your house."

"It's just a house."

"Well, you must have been an easy sale."

"My wife picked it."

"I'd like to meet her."

Cy nodded, making no promises. What would it be like with her if she knew his wife? That was ridiculous. Cy got down to business on the hit-and-run. He had had one adolescence, and he didn't want another.

The body of Stanley Collins had been found on a downtown street, parallel with Dirksen Boulevard. Not much open there at night except a couple of bars. There was the possibility that Collins had been in one of them, a possibility that Officer Agnes Lamb was checking out.

After lunch he looked over what had been found on the body—a wallet, a separate leather container for business cards, a pack of Marlboro Lights, a plastic lighter, keys, change, lint. Of course, there was the scarf that had been found on the front seat of his car. There was a handkerchief in a pocket of his suit jacket, along with a matchbook from the Rendezvous, one of the bars on the street where the body had been found.

There are bars and bars, the spectrum running from clean well-lighted places with windows through which to look in and look out to bistros where small lights embedded in the ceiling obscure rather than illumine the scene below them. The Rendezvous was of the ill-lit sort, but when Cy walked in, the door behind the bar was open and beyond that a door to the alley, where a truck was unloading supplies. The big guy behind the bar was a silhouette.

"What took you so long, Cy?"

"I recognize the voice but I can't see your face."

"You get used to it."

When he turned, light from behind revealed his face. "Perzel?"

Joe Perzel had been a cop for twenty years. Apparently tending bar was his retirement occupation.

"It's about Stanley Collins, right?"

"Where can we talk?"

"I got to keep an eye on that delivery."

"So let's go back there."

Perzel shrugged. "Okay. Anyone comes in, I'll see them."

"Who you expecting?"

"Customers. And the cops, of course."

"What do you know about the hit-and-run up the street?"

"When did it happen?"

"Last night."

"I work days. But I listened to the news this morning."

"And heard about Stanley Collins."

"The name jumped out at me."

"So you do know him?"

"He was a regular. Around the clock. Not a lush, he just liked the place. He did a lot of business here."

"Real estate?"

"Cell phones." Perzel made a face. "You know those hotels that have phones in the bathroom? Imagine getting a call from someone sitting on the pot. Nowadays a call could be coming from anywhere."

"Somebody ran over him, Joe."

"Last night?"

"Midnight or after."

"This street is pretty dark then."

"You know anybody who'd want to run over him?"

"Someone he sold a house to?" But Perzel let his pixie smile die. "No. He was full of bull, you know, but a nice guy. People liked him."

"I bought a house from him."

"Is this a confession?"

Cy was glad to get out of there, although he liked Joe Perzel. Or maybe because he did. Was some such future as that in store for him, tending bar? He'd rather be run over first.

3

It was the fate of David Jameson, D.D.S., to think of such phrases as "The spirit is willing but the flesh is weak" when his defenses against remembering the night at the Frosinone Hotel broke down and those bitter hours came flooding into his mind in all their humiliating detail. How absurd all his prudent precautions beforehand seemed. They would arrive in a rental car, he would pay cash, he would use an assumed name, no one would ever know that he and Phyllis had each finally succumbed to the attractions of the other and meant to anticipate the joys of matrimony in a rented bed.

"Compatibility is essential," Phyllis had assured him. "I know."

David did not want to know more. When he thought of possessing Phyllis it was a vague concept, something like a cloud enveloping her. And he would feel even more intensely the pleasure holding her in his arms gave him, her upper body pressed against his, her eyes looking up beseechingly. It was disconcerting that whenever he tried to kiss her, she opened her mouth. She might still be his patient. He kissed around its rims, missing the pressure of lips on lips.

"I do not want to make another mistake."

"You shall have children," he promised.

"Yes, that too. But first of all I want compatibility." She nibbled on his chin, standing on tiptoe to do it. She was such a little thing. He lifted her from the floor, and she squealed in delight. His eyes blurred at the thought of what lay before them at the hotel.

The first annoyance had been with the rental car. They would not take cash. It had to be a credit card. It was company policy. It was the policy of all the rental car companies except maybe Rent-a-Wreck. He turned over a credit card. That was no great problem. The point of the car was to protect their identity at the hotel.

Why the Frosinone? Phyllis had been surprised when he told her where they were going. Well, they couldn't saunter into the Hilton or the Radisson and count on not meeting someone they knew or, worse, being seen by but not seeing someone who knew them. He had heard of the Frosinone when he was in dental school as a place that accommodated couples when hotels were still snooty about whether a man and woman who showed up at the registration desk were married. Now, whenever David traveled, he was routinely asked how many keys to the room he wanted, as if he might make a trail of them like the colored beans in the story, and have a bevy of compliant females beating on his door. It was unlikely in the extreme that anyone at the Frosinone would recognize them.

"I think this is one of the hotels Stanley took his women to."

Phyllis said this when the rental car was parked in the hotel garage and they were ascending to the lobby in an elevator that seemed unsure whether it wanted to go up or sideways or maybe just straight down again. The mention of Stanley and his women was a blight on what they were doing, establishing a moral equivalence between Stanley Collins and David Jameson. For the first time Jameson fully realized what they had booked the room to do.

The arrangement had been made over time, little promissory notes from Phyllis when he had kissed around her open mouth while she emitted great sighs, made coy withdrawals followed by alarming advances, telling him that of course they could do nothing there in the house where she had lived with Stanley. Perhaps they should take a page from his book and just go off to a hotel. It had seemed so improbable at first that David had fallen in with the imaginary plan. Only, over time, as such talk became familiar, they seemed to have decided to do it. And now they had decided, and in the elevator she had said that this was a hotel where her husband had misbehaved. Suddenly, David was terrified at what lay ahead.

The swarthy little man at the desk looked at David as if he recognized him and he felt an impulse to take Phyllis's hand and dash back to the rented car.

"I can give you a suite." He made it sound like an indecent proposal. The name on his lapel was Primo Verdi.

Phyllis piped up, "Does it have a Jacuzzi?"

David was assailed by stories he had heard of hot sheet motels with mirrored ceilings and tubs for two.

"Just a shower."

David printed a false name on the form Verdi had slid toward him. "I'll need your credit card."

"I'll pay cash."

"The card is just in case of incidental expenses. Phone calls, room service . . ."

With the sense that all the precautions he had taken were rendered useless he handed the manager a credit card. A moment later, the data having been recorded, the card was handed back. It was like receiving evidence.

He fought the impulse to flee and call it quits because he had all the usual instincts of the male; he had known moments of lustful desire, even if he had always hitherto conquered them and been drawn back to thoughts of his vocation. An image of Father Dowling formed in his mind, memories came of their conversations, the topic of which had always been his putative vocation. It had been a pastoral instinct that had gotten him involved with Phyllis in the first place; he had wanted to give her the benefit of his knowledge of the canon law on marriage. He had not had to convince her that she really wasn't married, that a civil ceremony was not what the Church meant by marriage. He had meant to comfort, not seduce, her with this legal lore.

Registered, they crossed the lobby to the elevator.

"Pleasant dreams," Verdi called after them. He might have been taunting a bridegroom.

The sluggish elevator rose all too rapidly, stopped, and the door slid open. Phyllis took his hand and they started down the hall. She actually giggled and David was frozen with embarrassment. He had trouble with the key and she took it from him and got the door of their room opened. Inside, she tossed the shoulder bag she had brought onto the bed and threw her arms around him. When he bent to her, she swallowed him with her kiss. Then she pushed him away, picked up her bag, and said she'd only be a moment. Before she closed the bathroom door she whispered coyly, "Pull back the covers."

Then she was gone. He wanted to escape, but that was impossible. He could not bring her here and then just desert her. He waited, fully clothed, in an agony of indecision and guilt.

When she emerged she was wearing a nightie that fell no farther than the tips of her fingers. She hopped into bed and then looked at him.

"Undress."

"Phyllis . . ."

"I'll help you." She was on her feet again, and again she

giggled. It sounded horrible, a gurgle from hell. She was undoing his tie but he stopped her. Then she unbuckled his belt. He sprang back.

"No! Phyllis, this was a horrible mistake."

"Oh, come on. Don't be bashful."

Everything she said was wrong. How in the name of God had he got into such a situation? He dropped to his knees.

"What are you doing?"

"Praying."

Expressions came and went on her face but ended with a smile.

"All right, let's pray."

She knelt before him and again began to work at his belt. He slapped her hand, hard.

"Stop that!"

"What?"

"We have to go."

"David, we just got here." She rose to her feet and tried to lift him from his knees. "Everything will be all right. Come to bed."

He remembered the pathetic Padre Jose in Graham Greene's *Power and the Glory*, the faithless priest, teased by the neighboring kids who mimicked his woman when she called the apostate to bed.

He did sit on the bed then, and she sat beside him while he tried to explain that they must forget what they had been about to do. They had weakened but not fallen. They must remember that God could see them in the Frosinone, too. She listened in silence. Then she got off the bed and went back to the bathroom. When she came out again she was wearing her clothes.

"Let's go."

"Phyllis, I'm sorry."

"I know." But her voice was cold. How could he blame her?

An hour after they came to the hotel, they left. No need to

check out. He had paid in advance. But the manager watched them go with an amused expression. Perhaps he would think they were going out for dinner. The bed was mussed up, so the cleaning crew could think they had spent the night. He drove Phyllis home in the rental car, and they parted in silence.

The news of the hit-and-run death of Stanley Collins filled Bridget with foreboding. She had no way of knowing if others were aware of the relationship between David Jameson and Phyllis Collins, but such things were never secret for long. Of course, her own certainty that David was up to no good had been gained by the kind of snooping she would have deplored in anyone else. But her concern was for his own good, forget the ruined hope that he would some day learn to see her for the woman and person she was. Ever since Phyllis Collins had become a patient, David seemed to be spinning toward disaster. An affair with a married woman, and such a woman! The death of Stanley Collins, despite the fact that it was portrayed as an accident, seemed the conclusion of some intricate argument that had been formulating itself over the past weeks.

She had tried to write of these events in her diary, but after a few lines she stopped. How could any account spare her or fail to put her in the role of the rejected lovesick old maid? With little other than her hope to go on, she had persuaded herself that David would share her interests. The imagined future had been bathed in romantic tints, but the emphasis had been on their simply being together, enjoying music, discussing the books they had read. Bridget had gone into nursing for completely practical reasons, to finance her real life, her love of music and books. She had imagined David having a similarly pragmatic attitude toward his enormously successful practice. Surely he must be working himself so hard in order to free himself sooner for real life.

When she had spoken with Edna Hospers about David, girl to girl, hardly believing that she was confiding her most intimate secret, she had not pretended that David was interested in her. Of course, Edna had dismissed the thought that David could possibly not see the merits of his nurse.

"Don't doctors always marry nurses?" Edna asked.

"Some do."

"There you are. You have a running start."

So she had told Edna about Phyllis.

"You're kidding!"

"I wish I were."

"That woman is a complete airhead."

"Well, he finds her pneumatic enough. You know how she dresses."

Were men really such fools, a flash of flesh, a bit of bosom, and reason went out the window? Of course they were.

"But they get over it, Bridget. Anyway, she's already married."

"But will she stay that way?"

"He couldn't marry a divorced woman."

On such slender threads Bridget's hope depended. It was an infatuation from which David would recover, and when he did, faithful patient Bridget would be waiting for him. But the death of Stanley Collins changed everything.

When she heard of the accident on the radio while having breakfast, Bridget's first thought was that an obstacle had been removed from David's path. Now Phyllis Collins was unequivocally eligible. She had half a mind to call in sick. But then she wondered if David would cancel his appointments in order to console the widow, and she could not have kept away from the clinic.

"Has Dr. Jameson come in?" she asked Laura, a silly question given how early it was. But Laura's eyes rounded expressively.

"He's in his office," she whispered. "He was here when I got here."

That would have been half an hour ago. Laura arrived early in order, as she put it, to cook the books. The clock read 7:30. David was a creature of habit and usually entered on the stroke of eight, as reliable as a cuckoo clock.

There was a door through which David could emerge from his office into the room where the first of his trio of patients would be awaiting him. Bridget began noisily preparing for the day ahead, glancing at the door to see if he would look out to say good morning. But the closed door seemed to shut her out rather than shut him in. She went to it and knocked, moving her ear close to the panel. There was no indication that he was in there. Could Laura have been mistaken? Had she actually seen him? Bridget pushed open the door and looked into the darkened office. The light from behind her enabled her to see him seated at his desk.

"Are you all right?"

"Yes, of course. Turn on the light."

He blinked when she flipped the switch. He looked terrible.

"Have you been here all night?"

She actually looked around for signs that he had been drinking.

"What a question," he said, but his indignation died away, and he looked at her like a damned soul. She went swiftly to him and put her hand on his shoulder. To her surprise, he swung toward her and put his arms around her, laying his head on her breast. He burst into tears.

She held him tightly against her, rocking him gently. This was the fulfilment of four years of fantasy. Silence seemed the most effective form of communication. She ran her fingers through his hair while he sobbed.

How long did she hold him in her embrace, comforting him? Whatever was wrong with him, she could not believe that he was this upset over what had happened to Stanley Collins. She stepped back when he began to free himself. He looked up at her as if for the first time.

"You are a good, good woman," he said.

At the moment she wouldn't have minded stepping out of character. But there was no need to force the moment beyond what it already was. This was the beginning of something new between them.

"Have you had coffee?"

"I'd love some."

Laura turned questioningly while Bridget poured the coffee.

"Everything's all right, Laura."

David was on his feet when she went back to him. He seemed to have rinsed his face. He avoided meeting her eyes when he took the coffee. Now she wished she had urged him to talk while she held him in her arms. He was becoming his professional self and she could not bring herself to ask him what was the matter.

"Sometimes I feel like a stranger to myself," he said, his voice odd.

"I know what you mean."

"Oh, I doubt that." He did look at her then, soulfully, and Bridget felt placed on a pedestal.

"It was on the news," she said.

He gave her a puzzled look.

"Stanley Collins's accident."

"What accident?"

Well, that answered her question whether he was upset because he had heard of the hit-and-run.

"I didn't get the details," she lied. She did not want to talk about Stanley Collins because that would lead to talk of his silly wife.

"Who's my first patient?" he said, after a long silence.

David Jameson pressed his unshaven face against the chaste and starched bosom of his nurse and felt that he had returned to innocence. For a mad moment he imagined telling Bridget everything, confessing his sins to her, seeking readmission to the ranks of the righteous. But how could he tell anyone of that dreadful scene at the Frosinone?

He had been snatched from the jaws of serious sin. They both had. But Phyllis did not respond to his interpretation.

"Take me home."

He took her home. When she did look at him he felt that he had sinned by not sinning, and that robbed him of the sense of relief.

"I'm sorry, Phyllis."

"For what?" She turned sideways on the seat. "For making me feel cheap? For treating me as if I were some . . ." Her voice had risen and she was out of air before she could complete the sentence. She struck him on the arm, hard. Then she began to cry. She cried all the way home.

"Would you like me to come in?"

"No!"

She got out of the car and he scrambled from his side, determined to walk her to the door like a good date. But she ran to the front door and was behind the screen when he got there.

"Phyllis . . ."

"Good night," she hissed. "Good-bye." And she shut the inner door with a bang.

Going back to his rented car, he wavered between regret and the thought that this was a definitive breach, that the interlude of dalliance with Phyllis Collins was at last behind him, through no merit of his own. The second thought was stronger as he drove away. No longer would he waste the daytime hours thinking of Phyllis, wanting to protect her from the cruel fate that had befallen her, rescue her from her husband and make her his own. He knew what others made of his infatuation with Phyllis. Bridget had been explicit at first until he silenced her. Even Laura smiled her disappoval. As for Father Dowling, David had sensed the change in the priest's attitude, though no damning word had issued from him. How could Father Dowling take his clerical aspirations seriously? Would he have laughed if told that David was engaged in pastoral work of a sort? Wednesday after Wednesday he had spent counseling Phyllis, feeding the hope that she could rid herself of Stanley and be in good standing with the Church. It had been a species of wooing. Who knows what might have happened by now if Amos Cadbury had not cast such a pall over things. For Phyllis to leave Stanley—or vice versa—was for her to be cut off from his eventual inheritance. It had been professionally risky for him to assume the role of mediator, going with her to the lawyer's office. And Amos Cadbury was a friend of Father Dowling's! David felt that he had been in the grip of some madness and was now free.

But other and contradictory thoughts came, perhaps elicited by the lingering aroma of Phyllis's perfume in the car. The rented car. His own was parked in a downtown garage, a block from the car rental office on Bailey Street. Getting rid of the car seemed an imperative, to purge his mind of all reminders of the humiliation in the Frosinone. But when he drove down Bailey he saw the lighted sign of the Rendezvous and, on an impulse, pulled into the lot. This was the nightclub that Stanley allegedly frequented. In Phyllis's account it had acquired almost mythical status as a den of iniquity. Having emerged unscathed from the fire of temptation and adultery with Phyllis, he would toast his intact status with a drink at her husband's favorite bar.

It was not at all what he expected. He had been ready for nudes writhing on a stage surrounded by slavering men urging them on to depravity. But the Rendezvous was sedate, a place of worship where sentimentality in the form of tried and true ballads was celebrated. A throaty rendition of "Happy Days Are Here Again," sung in a lenten tempo that negated the sunny optimism of the words, accompanied David to an empty stool at the bar. The singer had the full attention of the patrons, and David felt as if he were arriving late at church. Soon David Jameson was among the worshipers.

Dignity in passion, that was the phrase he settled on to describe the singer's voice, which, while remaining the same, altered subtly as she went through her repertoire, illumined by a spotlight, pouring out her heart to an anonymous invisible crowd. Then he realized that this was the woman of whom Phyllis had spoken so bitterly as the reason for her husband's sudden interest in the Church's marriage laws. David felt drawn to her himself, almost impersonally, as if she were a force, a passion untouched by thought, primeval. He sipped the beer he had ordered to rid himself of the distraction of the bartender. Too soon it was over, the lights went up slightly, and the singer was gone.

David looked around. Was Stanley Collins here? The mirror behind the bar was obscured by an array of bottles. Conversation rose but was still somehow hushed and reverent. Someone slipped onto the stool beside him and a half-full glass of bourbon was placed before the man. He drank from the glass as if it were beer then smiled at David.

"*Ciao.*"

"*Buenos noches.*"

The little man laughed. His long fingers lay on the bar as if he were about to elicit music from it.

"You're the accompanist."

A nod.

"She's wonderful."

"None better."

The atmosphere of the bar encouraged familiarity. "Do you know Stanley Collins?"

The little man turned toward him. "Are you a detective?"

Detective! He felt oddly flattered, as if such a profession, better than that of dentist, belonged to this place. He smiled enigmatically.

"He's a sonofabitch," the little man said.

This was said matter-of-factly. It was the view of her husband, differently expressed, that he had heard from Phyllis. The little man tossed off what remained of his drink and pushed his glass forward for a refill. The bartender swiftly accommodated him.

"A general or a particular sonofabitch?"

"Both."

"Where is he?"

"Pestering Wanda in her dressing room."

The little man was distracted by a conversation on the other side of him. He drank as if it were a secret his hand kept from him, the glass lifting once, twice, and after the third time pushed forward empty. David got his attention to get directions to the men's room.

Moving among the tables, he told himself no one would recognize him in that subdued if brighter lighting. The restroom was at the end of a long hallway lined with doors on one of which was lettered WANDA. His pace slowed. Stanley Collins was in there. Lurid images teased his mind, but he continued to his destination. The face that looked at him from the mirror did not reveal what he had recently been through at the Frosinone, looking innocently back at him, the face of one who thought he had a vocation.

He got out his cell phone and retreated into a booth where he dialed Phyllis's number. It rang and rang but finally she answered.

"Phyllis, we have to talk."

"Talk is the one thing you're good at."

"I can't tell you how sorry I am."

"So why call?"

"I'm coming over."

"Where are you?"

He hesitated. "The Rendezvous."

"The Rendezvous!"

"He's here."

"So you're both there. Isn't that fitting?" She was crying.

"The piano player says he's a sonofabitch."

"I wish he were dead."

For a second he thought she meant the piano player.

He would have liked to stay, to listen to more songs by Wanda, but that seemed vaguely untrue to Phyllis. He went up the street to the parking lot and his rented car.

* * *

The following morning, after working on six patients he told Bridget to cancel the rest of his appointments. Her expression told him how unprecedented this was. But he could not forget that Phyllis needed him now more than ever. Who else did she have? Surely she would see this?

"They're already in the waiting room."

"Can't a dentist be sick?"

"You look it."

He might have shaved before his first appointment, but at the moment that had not seemed important. Bridget's report of the news she had heard on the radio changed everything. It seemed self-indulgent to pretend that it was a day like any other.

When Phyllis came to the door, she fell into his arms, and he backed her into the house.

"I knew you would come."

"Of course."

Her mouth remained closed when she lifted it to his kiss. The nonsense at the Frosinone was behind them.

When David Jameson called at the rectory Father Dowling could hear Marie asking him if this was his day off.

"Wednesdays," he said in sepulchral tones.

It was Friday. Marie opened the study door.

"It's Dr. Jameson!" Marie's eyes met the pastor's, their lidded comment negating the lilt in her voice.

Jameson entered and sat and stared at Father Dowling. The door shut slowly.

"Father, I have an unusual request."

Had he finally decided to take the plunge and enter a seminary? Father Dowling looked receptive. He would write an equivocal letter of recommendation.

"Phyllis Collins would like her husband's funeral to be at St. Hilary's."

"Ah."

"Neither one of them has practiced the faith for years. She is coming around, I think, but in his case . . . But I shouldn't gossip about the dead. The thing is, they have no parish."

"She asked you to request this?"

He nodded. "She is out in the car if you would like to speak to her. I am taking her to McDivitt's Funeral Home."

"That's where the body is?"

"Yes."

"I know McDivitt. I'll work it out with him. Tell her it's all right. The funeral can be on Monday morning."

"Can there be a rosary?"

"Sunday night at McDivitt's."

Jameson was on his feet, a relieved expression having replaced that of funereal concern. "I knew you would. I told Phyllis you would."

At the door, Jameson was still so elated he forgot to ask for a blessing before hurrying out to his car. A dark figure sat in the passenger seat.

"What's it got to do with him?" Marie asked and Father Dowling turned.

"I hope you didn't have your ear to the door of the study."

"He told me, he just blurted it out when I went to the door. Are you going to do it?"

"What would you advise?"

"Oh, stop it. I knew you would."

"I am going to have to soundproof the study."

"The noise doesn't bother me," Marie said, and headed grandly toward her kitchen, getting through the swinging door before the last word was stolen from her.

Over the years, McDivitt's establishment had acquired an ecumenical éclat that did not exclude agnostics or even the openly irreligious. There were as many mansions in McDivitt's as we are told there are in the kingdom of heaven, and while the bulk of his business was Catholic, McDivitt had never turned away a customer. Strange rites had been performed in some of the viewing rooms: a medicine man had danced soundlessly in his moccasins, a light-footed witch had stepped among strange symbols on the floor chanting unintelligibly, at the services of a notorious atheist as a weeping friend cursed God from the podium. Nothing altered the benign sadness with which McDivitt presided over his establishment. Ashes to ashes, dust to dust. He had not invented this grim truth about the end of earthly life but he was prepared to soften its effect on the bereaved.

"Will it be here or in the church, Father?"

"The church. A funeral Mass."

McDivitt's hair was snow white, reminiscent of the cotton pulled from aspirin bottles. His matching brows lifted slightly over his dark-rimmed glasses.

"Was he a parishioner?"

"His parents were."

"Of course! I remember them. They died together. I thought I had seen Stanley Collins before."

"When you buried his parents?"

"Of course, he was younger then." McDivitt paused. "And alive."

"He called on me recently."

"A sad ending. But he will look just fine at the wake."

"No one can excel you."

"You're kind to say so, Father. It is not a work that receives many compliments. Not that one expects them."

On the wall of McDivitt's office were various certificates and awards. One from a professional association of undertakers. A lifetime achievement award.

"Praise from your peers must be all the sweeter then."

McDivitt looked morosely at the award that had caught Father Dowling's eye. "Someone told them I meant to retire."

"Even so."

"Did you know Father Hug?"

"The Franciscan?"

"Yes."

"He was pastor at the time." The cottony eyebrows met in disapproval. "That man actually tried to talk young Collins into a single casket."

"For both parents?"

"Barbaric. And he wouldn't let up. But I prevailed." The frown returned. "Up to a point. They share the same grave."

A moment of silence sufficed to restore McDivitt's professional expression.

"The wake will be on Sunday. I'll lead the rosary."

"Good, good." But then McDivitt would have reacted in the same way if told that an ox would be sacrificed and wine spilt as an oblation. No, that wasn't fair. Imagine spending your life among the dead.

Although Marie approved of Father Dowling's decision—the dead deserved the benefit of the doubt if anyone did—in her heart of hearts she had misgivings. It reminded her of the antinomian reign of the Franciscans when notorious sinners had been canonized from the pulpit when they were buried. Recent events had brought back the Collinses' funeral when Father Pacific had actually condemned the excessive expenditures for the departed.

"One in life, they should be united in death. Before this altar they gave their hands to one another, and the hand of God reached down and took them to himself at the same moment. Why should what God joined together be separated even in death?"

An odd sermon from beginning to end, but that was the rule with Pacific. In any case, the couple had been model Catholics, and the church was happily full for their exit. Their son was another kettle of fish, apparently. Marie had picked up rumors, from Maud Pinske of all people, who showed up for Mass on Sunday and took Marie aside.

"Is it true that Stanley Collins will be buried from St. Hilary's?"

"It was in the paper."

"I suppose it's best."

Marie bristled. Father Dowling's decisions did not require the approval of Amos Cadbury's secretary.

"Mr. Cadbury is so pleased."

That was a different story. Marie nodded.

"Of course, you know what he was like?"

"Mr. Cadbury?"

"Marie!"

"Come over to the rectory and have a cup of tea."

A troubled marriage, that was the burden of Maud's story. Listening, urging her on, Marie thought of the separate visits of Phyllis and Stanley Collins to Father Dowling. They had both made a point of the pastor's degree in canon law and experience on the archdiocesan marriage tribunal. Against the background of Maud Pinske's sibilant confiding this took on a new significance.

"The two of them actually consulted Mr. Cadbury, Marie."

"The Collinses?"

"No. No. She and the other man."

"About . . ."

"They claimed that there hadn't been a real marriage."

"And she had already found a replacement?"

"A dentist." Maud patted her thin lips with a napkin.

"No!"

"Jameson." Maud said the name soundlessly, her lips enunciating in an exaggerated way.

"David Jameson!" It was all Marie could do not to take Maud in her arms and give her a pacific hug.

"You know him?"

"I think so," Marie said carefully. Already she was thinking of how she could convey this to Father Dowling in a way that would not seem to be gossiping.

Throughout Sunday, Marie had nursed the new knowledge that she had received. David Jameson came to the eleven o'clock Mass, making a point of being seen, taking a long time to sit and get settled in the front pew. Drumming up business? He did run a larger-than-average ad in the parish bulletin: Smile and the World Smiles with You. Everything about the man seemed to confirm Marie's longstanding dislike. Pharisee, she thought. But with the thought came a self-referential accusation. She brought her hand to her breast and begged God for forgiveness. She said a prayer for the repose of Stanley Collins's soul, but that was further distraction, given what Maud had told her. When Dr. Jameson returned to his pew after receiving communion, hands folded like an altar boy, eyes down, a reverent expression on his pale face, Marie murmured, "Behold the bridegroom cometh." And again she beat her breast in contrition.

After lunch they counted the collection, and Marie was about to climb the back stairs to her apartment for a well-deserved nap when Phil Keegan showed up to watch a televised game with the pastor.

"You money changers finished?"

"All done," Father Dowling said cheerfully. "I suppose you want a beer."

"Is the Pope Polish?"

Phil mentioned another game that began at six and Father Dowling shook his head. "I have a wake, Phil."

"That's too bad."

"Stanley Collins," Marie said.

"Come on." Phil turned to Father Dowling. "Was he a parishioner?"

"The family was."

"We're not so sure his death was an accident, Roger."

"Come into the study, Phil."

But Marie was not going to be cut out of this. "Why not?"

"It's a long and gory story. And inconclusive. Agnes Lamb has turned up something that suggests the accident was deliberate, and Cy thinks she may be right."

"You mean he might have been killed?"

"Don't call the paper and television station, Marie. It may be nothing."

"What is it?"

"Stanley was quite a ladies' man. And, of course, his wife did not approve. Agnes is thinking of that case in Texas."

"The dentist's wife?" Marie cried.

"You probably know more about it than I do, Marie."

"What would I know about dentists?"

"He might have been run down by his own car."

Marie let out a little shriek, more of morbid delight than shock.

Amos Cadbury had grown old, distinguished, and wealthy in the practice of the law in Fox River, but now, in his eighth decade, he was disinclined to rest on his laurels. The truth was that there was often the taste of dust and ashes in his mouth. As a student at Notre Dame, he had made regular visits to the grotto, often on his way to St. Mary's College, which was reached by a road flanked by giant trees that whispered their benediction overhead, past the community cemetery where, under rows of identical crosses, the deceased members of the congregation who had given their lives to Notre Dame lay awaiting the last trump, across the highway, and onto the St. Mary's campus. Obtaining a wife from the student body of St. Mary's College was not guaranteed to every Notre Dame student, but then the enrollment numbers were disproportional. The competition for the young ladies was correspondingly fierce but civil. Amos had found his soul mate in his junior year, became formally engaged to her at graduation, and married her when he finished law school. They had lived a long and happy if fruitless marriage, but now Amos was alone, against all the actuarial tables the survivor, and long thoughts came easily to him.

As a young man, the austere ideals of the law had seemed to Amos a bulwark against disorder and chaos, and so to some degree they were. But however noble the law, lawyers and judges were men and their blindfolds were often loosened by lesser motives than justice. Now that the shadows had lengthened, he let his partners bring in new business while he himself increasingly attended to the estates of departed clients. Death did not dissolve his duty to them, and he was determined that their wills should be fulfilled. Even when, as in the case of Frederick Collins, he had not entirely approved of the provisions.

"I do not want to put a large sum of money into Stanley's hands," Frederick had said in his soft voice, and his wife Jessica had nodded assent. "The boy is given to folly, and unless he has to earn his bread he will become foolish indeed."

"You mean to disinherit him?"

"Oh, no. Perhaps I am simply putting off the evil day, but I do not want him to come into his inheritance until he is fifty years old."

"Fifty years old," Amos repeated carefully.

"Even that may be too soon."

Amos was not completely surprised at the amount the Collinses had amassed. Frederick and Jessica had lived abstemiously and invested with imagination as well as prudence.

Amos had drawn up the will as desired, not telling Frederick that his son would almost certainly contest it when the facts were made known to him. The reading of the will occurred much sooner than the Collinses or Amos would have guessed. The suddenness of their deaths was an argument for drawing up a will in good time. With almost equal surprise, Stanley accepted his father's decision.

"It will eventually be mine, won't it, Mr. Cadbury?"

"Without any doubt. I have never drawn up a will that has been broken."

"I'll think of it as an insurance policy."

"Of course, it will amount to a good deal more by the time you inherit."

Stanley was then in his late twenties, halfway to affluence. Whether he simply shared his parents' distrust of his practical wisdom or just liked the idea of a pot at the end of his personal rainbow Amos was never sure. Whatever the cause, he was glad that Stanley had not been given bad advice and attempted to break his father's will to obtain his inheritance immediately. He would have lost such an effort, Amos had no doubt of that. And so the matter had remained until two recent events.

One afternoon Maud announced that the ineffable Tuttle had shown up without an appointment and wished to discuss a mutual client with Amos Cadbury.

"A mutual client?"

Maud nodded. If nothing else, this brazen and preposterous claim piqued Amos's curiosity. There was no limit to the breaches to permissible legal conduct that Tuttle could devise.

"I will see him."

Tuttle had removed his tweed hat before coming in, and his unbuttoned topcoat flapped about him like a seedy academic gown. Amos bowed at a chair and Tuttle collapsed into it.

"I believe you represent Stanley Collins."

Amos gave the slightest of nods but remained silent.

"So do I."

There was a note of triumph in Tuttle's voice, and given what he went on to say, Amos could not begrudge it to him. If the scruffy little lawyer was right, Stanley Collins had finally grown impatient waiting for his inheritance and had decided to go to a lawyer about it. It pained Amos that Stanley had not spoken to him first.

Tuttle said, "He wanted to come to you himself, but I advised against it."

"It might have saved a good deal of time."

"I have read the will."

"It cannot be broken, Tuttle. I assure you of that."

Tuttle lifted a hand. "I wouldn't suggest that, not in a million years. I have another proposal."

The proposal was that Amos arrange for regular payments to Stanley to be charged against his eventual inheritance.

"You want me to break the will myself?"

"It's a matter of interpretation."

"When I draw up a will, Mr. Tuttle, I take pains that 'interpretation,' as you call it, will be kept to a minimum. The will contains the wishes of my clients, stated as clearly as could be, and in a completely unequivocal fashion. For me to do as you suggest would be to flaunt the wishes of a client."

"You're trustee of the money, aren't you?"

This, too, was a matter of public knowledge. "Yes."

"The amount must have grown over the years."

"I would be a poor trustee if it hadn't."

"So, just considering the money that has been made since the will was drawn up—"

Cadbury stopped him. Even to discuss such sharp practice was painful to him. He stood.

"Thank you, Mr. Tuttle, for coming to see me."

"I may be back."

Amos smiled. In a well-ordered world Tuttle would have been disbarred long ago. The fact that Stanley Collins had gone to such a man seemed to corroborate his parents' estimate of his intelligence. Nonetheless, it was irksome that Stanley had not come to him to discuss his discontents.

It was the following week that David Jameson had called for an appointment. Maud was suggesting a date some months in the future, but Amos passing through the outer office happened to overhear. When he glanced at the name Maud had jotted down, he indicated that he would take the phone.

"Dr. Jameson? Amos Cadbury. How might I help you?"

He arranged to see Jameson the following morning. There was a woman with him.

"Is this Mrs. Jameson?"

This simple question threw both Jameson and his companion into consternation. She began to identify herself, speaking to Maud, and Jameson himself said that that was why they had come to him. Now Amos was himself confused and not a little curious. He got them settled into chairs and sat looking receptively at them. Maud had withdrawn.

"Mrs. Collins has come to me and told me a number of things and I offered to accompany her here. It has to do with her husband's inheritance."

"I see."

"She is a patient of mine."

Amos nodded. Mrs. Collins simpered. Something about their togetherness caused Amos unease. Why would a dentist bring a patient to a lawyer to discuss her husband's inheritance? The reason eventually emerged. Mrs. Collins was afraid that her husband was contemplating divorce.

"Where does that put me?"

"I don't understand."

"Stanley always made a big thing of the money awaiting him. Sometimes I think it kept us together." She said this without embarrassment. "If he should divorce me . . ."

"His inheritance is not due to come to him for some time."

"She would be cut off?" Jameson asked.

"She could hardly be cut off from what is not yet in possession of her husband."

"I wouldn't get a dime," Mrs. Collins cried. "I knew it."

"Now Phyllis." Jameson turned to Amos. "There must be some way in which she can lay claim to some portion of the money that was in effect promised her from the time she married."

"You are not a lawyer, Dr. Jameson, or you would not imagine such an imperative."

He spelled it out. Take a couple who divorced. Some years later, one or the other came into a sum of money. That money could hardly be regarded as part of any settlement since at the time of divorce, ex hypothesi, it did not belong to the person in question. He explained this again, in several ways, but the lay mind is ill equipped to understand that the law does not obey what the lay mind regards as common sense.

"Have you no advice at all?"

Amos hesitated, then launched into the deep. "Reconcile with your husband, Mrs. Collins. Chase thoughts of divorce from his mind. In a few years . . ."

She burst into angry tears. With an effort and after several unsuccessful attempts, Jameson got her to her feet and led her to the door.

"Thank you for seeing us, Mr. Cadbury," he said.

"Thanks for nothing," cried Phyllis Collins.

When they were gone, Maud looked in, but Amos waved her wearily away. He turned in his chair and looked out at the skyline of Fox River. Mark Twain told the story of how his family had been ruined by pinning their hopes constantly on some land in Tennessee that would eventually come their way. Had Frederick Collins unwittingly done the same to his son? And to his ill-tempered little wife toward whom David Jameson exhibited such considerate tenderness?

The following week Stanley Collins was run down by a car. Amos considered it a professional obligation to attend the wake and funeral. An obligation to old Frederick Collins, whose own joint funeral with his wife had been such a fiasco.

Cy Horvath told his wife he was going to attend Stanley Collins's wake.

"Who's he?"

"He sold us this house."

"You want to make sure he's dead?"

"I thought you liked this house."

"Just kidding."

"He's dead all right. I was there for the autopsy."

"Ugh."

"You don't have to go."

"Neither do you."

"I know."

"I don't even remember what he looks like."

So he went alone to McDivitt's and took a seat in back. It was a pretty good turnout. Someone sat down beside him, and he was surprised to see it was Joe Perzel. Joe punched his arm and tried to look solemn.

"Night off, Joe?"

"I work days."

"I thought you were a cop."

Joe groaned. It was an old joke, and a bad one. "Where does your dad work?" "He doesn't work. He's a cop."

"There's Keegan."

And so it was. He came in with Father Dowling and McDivitt. McDivitt stopped just inside the door. Father Dowling continued to the prie-dieu in front of the open coffin. Phil noticed Cy and Perzel and joined them, grunting as he sat. Then the rosary began.

The rosary takes fifteen minutes in such circumstances, the priest saying the first half of the prayers, everyone else doing the second half. Five mysteries. Phil had fished a rosary from his pocket, Cy kept count on his fingers, Perzel seemed to be dozing. Usually when Cy came to a wake it was to check out the crowd because they were working on a case. Well, maybe Stanley Collins was a case. Not that there was a big chance they would find the one who ran him down. Probably some car thief who had panicked and then returned the car where he had found it. Cy thought about it. Somewhere someone was sweating it out, wondering if he would be tracked down. It happened. Some nosey neighbor notices the damage to his car, or the culprit made the mistake of taking it in too soon for repair and a mechanic put two and two together. Except in this case, they had the car and it belonged to Stanley Collins. Even so, whoever had driven it would be a nervous wreck.

The widow was in the front row, in black, a miniskirt. One of those gauzy black things over her head. Mantilla. Who was the guy next to her? Cy whispered the question to Phil.

"A dentist named Jameson."

"Like the whiskey?"

"I guess."

Well, he was a tall drink of water, anyway. Most of the people Cy didn't know, and that seemed an excuse for sticking around afterward. Phil seemed to know a lot of them. Of course, Cy knew Amos Cadbury.

"Many are parishioners from St. Hilary's," Phil said.

"That his parish?"

"More or less."

Why else would Dowling be in charge? Perzel was talking to a nervous overweight guy in a loud sport jacket. Cy joined them.

"This is George Sawyer."

"Stanley and I are partners. Were," he corrected.

"Sawyer and Collins."

"That's right."

"You sold me my house."

Sawyer looked at him quickly. This was no place to talk with a dissatisfied client.

"Any problems?"

"Yeah. I'm not there enough. Helluva way for your partner to die."

Sawyer shook his head. "I will miss him."

"Too bad the driver didn't."

Sawyer walked away. He had spoken in solemn tones and didn't care for Cy's crack. Cy didn't care for it too much himself.

Amos Cadbury took Father Dowling away, and Phil suggested they all go for a drink.

"How about the Rendezous?" Perzel said.

"Where's that?" Phil asked.

"I'll show you." Someone passed them, and Joe called out, "Hey, Wanda. Hi."

Wanda was a lot of woman with enough hair on her head for several more. But her eyes were red and tears flowed down her cheeks. She had to blink to get Joe into focus. Then she took him in her arms and began to sob. Nobody was more surprised than Joe. He looked over her head at Cy with a silly pleased expression.

"We work together," he explained. He spoke into her hair; he had little choice. "Wanda, we're going for a drink. Come on along."

She stepped back and looked at him with anger. "Now? Tonight?" She didn't hit Joe, although she seemed to consider it. They all watched her leave, a treat in itself.

"You work with her, Joe?"

"That is Wanda Janski," Joe said, as if they should have known. "She sings at the Rendezvous."

"But not tonight."

"You heard her."

"So let's go somewhere we can see one another."

At that hour, the sports bar across from the courthouse was all but empty. They took a booth and ordered a couple pitchers of beer. When those were gone, they ordered another. Joe didn't drink much. "I see too much of it."

That left a lot of beer for Cy and Phil. On the third round, Agnes Lamb came in, sober as a probation officer. She pulled up a chair. Joe, who was a bit of a racist, decided to have a glass of beer after all. A mistake. After three glasses, his tongue was thick, and he wouldn't shut up.

"I knew the guy. He drank at my bar. He was, well, not a friend exactly, but someone I knew. That makes it different. It hits you, someone you knew . . ."

"Who's he talking about?" Agnes asked.

"Stanley Collins."

"Did Cy tell you we found the car, Captain?"

"Where?" Joe asked.

"In the parking lot at some dive called the Rendezvous."

"Dive," Joe protested. "I work there."

"Sorry."

"His car?"

Agnes nodded. "Pour me another."

"Right there in the parking lot?" Joe asked.

"Not twenty-five yards from where the body was found."

"What do you make of that?"

Agnes thought about it. "I don't think he was driving it."

The talk around the press room at the courthouse was of the way Stanley had been killed, and Bob Oliver wondered how many of the reporters knew that the victim was his brother-in-law. It wasn't something he had bragged about.

"It wasn't a hit-and-run," Tetzel said in an authoritative voice.

"He didn't get hit by a car?"

"Sure he did. But it was his own car."

Everybody began to talk at once. Bob Oliver left unobtrusively while Tetzel's pronouncement had everyone's attention.

He took the elevator to the main floor and then walked around the rotunda, thinking. Which meant he was going around in circles, literally and metaphorically. His first thought was of Phyllis. God knew she had reason enough to run Stanley over. If it came to that, and if she was brought to trial, she would probably get a standing ovation from the jury when they found out how Stanley catted around.

Something Verdi had said to him displaced this thought. The manager of the Frosinone had walked into Luigi's the other night with Flora on his arm and he seemed to steer her in Oliver's direction.

"How's the intrepid reporter?"

Oliver was trying not to look at Flora.

"This is my wife," Verdi said, and he might have been a crowing rooster.

"Hi," Flora said, and her manner seemed to promise professional discretion.

"My third wife, to be exact."

"It's best to be exact."

Was the idiot serious? But Verdi was dumb enough to marry one of the escort girls who worked out of the Frosinone.

"Congratulations."

"Oh, we're divorced," Flora chirped.

"Which is it, Verdi?"

"Both." Why was the manager grinning?

"We've met," Oliver said.

"I know."

And off they went to a table where the sound of their laughter had rankled Oliver.

Oliver had left his unfinished drink and got out of there. Now, in the rotunda of the courthouse, he decided to pay a visit to Verdi. Tuttle hung around the Frosinone, and it occurred to him that Verdi was capable of saying something to the lawyer.

"You still thinking of writing up this place?" Primo Verdi said when Bob came to the registration desk of the Frosinone.

"We have a family readership."

"I thought you were interested in architecture."

"This place is an architectural ruin."

"I finally read your piece about the dentist."

Bob looked at him.

"Nice photographs. That's how I recognized him."

"Jameson?"

"He's a patron."

"Of this dump? You must have mistaken him for someone else."

"Well, he did sign the register as Jones. We get a lot of Joneses here. I doubt the lady with him was Mrs. Jones."

"Yeah?"

"One of those women trying to look like a kid, you know? Hair streaked, miniskirt, blouse half unbuttoned. Nice smile, though."

This word portrait of Phyllis filled him with anger. Was Verdi putting him on? But how could he have gotten such an accurate version of Phyllis? It was the thought that she had come to the Frosinone with Jameson that angered him. Stanley would have dropped her in a minute if he had known of it.

"When was this?"

Verdi thought, and then consulted his computer. "Thursday."

"Last Thursday?"

"Last Thursday."

"The bar open? I'll buy you a drink."

"At eleven-thirty?"

"What are you, a Methodist?"

The bar was open, if empty. At his station, the bartender looked like the Maytag repairman. He brightened up when he saw that his boss was bringing in a customer. Bob ordered a Bloody Mary, and Verdi told the bartender he would have his regular, which turned out to be a foamy brandy Alexander when the drinks were put on their table.

"A habit I picked up in Vegas."

"I can't stand that town."

"It's where I met my third wife."

"The one you divorced?"

"I divorced them all. The course of true love never runs smooth."

"Tell me about Jameson and the woman."

"What's to tell? We don't have security cameras in the rooms. Actually, I gave them a suite."

Verdi's smirk was more than annoying. It occurred to Bob that Verdi was Phyllis's alibi, if she should need one. But what a story. I was in a suite at the Frosinone with my dentist when my husband was run over. Now that the police had decided it wasn't a routine hit-and-run, a picture of Phyllis could appear on television and in the paper. If Verdi saw it and made the connection, what might he do? Primo Verdi was a menace. And just when Phyllis seemed home free, rid of Stanley and due to come into a fortune.

Verdi wiped foam from his lips. "So what brings you here?"

The question caught Bob off guard. He brought his drink to his lips, trying to think of a plausible story.

"Flora is semiretired, Oliver, but there are others."

How long had it been since he blushed? It was bad enough to know that he had availed himself of one of the Frosinone escorts, but for Primo Verdi to know was something else. Who knew what resentment he felt at men who had squired Flora?

"You're a lucky man, Verdi."

"Some luck is bad."

"It will be our secret."

It was a question. To Bob Oliver's momentary relief, Verdi nodded and lifted his foamy drink. But after he left, the thought of trusting the discretion of Primo Verdi was disturbing. After all, it was the fear that Verdi would tell Tuttle about Bob Oliver and the Frosinone escorts that had decided him to pay a visit to the manager. The result was at best equivocal.

Tuttle had been avoiding his office since the body of Stanley Collins was found. It was dangerous there in the daytime, with Hazel around. His big mistake had been to tell her what a killing he was going to make on Stanley Collins. He would take Amos Cadbury to the cleaners. His client and his shrewd lawyer could live in ease for the rest of their lives on the settlement Tuttle would wangle out of Cadbury. He had expected the icy reception the first time. He knew what Cadbury thought of him. Well, maybe if he had been born with a silver spoon in his mouth he could have become a lawyer like Amos Cadbury. But Tuttle had crawled his way up from the bottom, not too far from the bottom, sustained by the unflagging trust of his paternal parent.

Law school had been almost a career in itself for Tuttle. Most courses he had taken at least twice before he passed, and getting by the bar exam had required him to have sleeves full of little reminders of this and that. Tuttle senior had been prouder than Tuttle when, at last, success was attained. He then expired, as if the point of his life had been achieved. He was commemorated in the title of the firm, Tuttle & Tuttle. People often asked who the other Tuttle was. Sometimes it was enough just to say, "My father."

To those who knew him too well, Tuttle would say he was schizoid. "One of us is manic, the other depressive." But his father's place on the door was no joke to Tuttle. Tears would come to his eyes when he remembered his father's trust in him, the sacrifices he had made for him, the pride he had taken in having a son who was a lawyer.

He could tell Peanuts Pianone about his father. But then you could tell Peanuts anything. Every day was a new world for Peanuts, and his spot on the Fox River police force was a triumph of nepotism. His uncle had taken the exams for him, the one who was now in Leavenworth. Peanuts was on a perpetual roving assignment, meaning he was to keep out of the way, take his check, and not bother anyone. Peanuts and Tuttle were fast friends.

"Fire her," Peanuts said, when Tuttle told him he couldn't go to his office because Hazel was there.

"I don't like scenes."

"Who's the boss?"

Good question, and not one he would want to put to a vote with Hazel in the room. So he kept clear of the office, going in when night had fallen to see what was new. There was a note on his desk, written in Hazel's unmistakable hand.

"Nice going, jackass!"

Well, what prophet was honored in his own country, or what lawyer in his own office? Thoughts of Amos Cadbury worried the edges of his mind. Ah well, you had to play the hand you were dealt.

Sitting in his unlit office as the sounds of night traffic lifted from below, Tuttle reviewed the situation, looking for some way to redeem his efforts. Stanley was out of the picture, poor devil, nailed by a hit-and-run driver, doubtless in his cups, probably both of them were. Through Peanuts, he had gotten the slim file on the case. No one seemed particularly anxious to pursue it, willing to write it off as the collateral damage of modern civilization. Then he thought of Stanley's widow.

He found the number in the book and dialed it. A man answered.

"Mrs. Collins, please."

"Who is calling?

"This is Tuttle. The lawyer. I represented her husband in an effort to get at the inheritance that was left him."

"Her husband?"

"Stanley."

"I don't think she would want to talk to you."

"Why don't we let her decide? Who is this?"

"A friend."

Stanley had confided that his wife was running around with a dentist. That was why he wanted to unload her. Tuttle had not encouraged this at the time. He didn't handle divorces, a bargain with his sainted father who was a champion of hearth and home, God bless him. What was the name? Guinness? Powers?

"Is this Dr. Jameson?"

There was a significant silence. "How did you know that?"

"I told you I was Stanley's lawyer."

An experienced angler could feel the tug on the line. Tuttle gave it a little jerk.

"Maybe the three of us should meet."

"The funeral is tomorrow."

"I will be there, of course."

"Well . . ."

"See you then."

He put down the phone and closed his eyes, breathing a

prayer to his father, certain that it had been his inspiration that led him to remember the name Jameson. He had half a mind to leave a note for Hazel. He rejected the idea. He had run aground before by anticipating triumph. This time he would be Mr. Cool until the fish was landed. He put his feet on the desk, tipped his tweed hat over his eyes and drifted into sleep.

He was awakened by a shrill voice.

"Did you sleep here!"

Tuttle scrambled awake, setting his chair in motion. It shot away from the desk, hit the wall, and dumped him on the floor. He got to his feet.

"It's about time you got here." He looked at his watch. "I have to get to a funeral."

"Your own by the looks of you."

Tuttle had an electric razor in his desk that if used carefully was safe. It did have a way of grabbing hold of whiskers and not letting go. He plugged it in and turned it on. A whining sound filled the office.

"You need a shower," Hazel said.

"I don't have time."

"Whose funeral?"

"Stanley Collins's."

"Your late client." Hazel spoke with disdain.

"I am now in contact with the widow."

Hazel was impressed despite herself.

"What good is she?"

"The heir of the heir."

"What time is the funeral?"

"Ten."

"Go home and clean up. I'll drive you . . ."

But Tuttle got past her and into the outer office. "My car is parked on the street."

"If it hasn't been ticketed and towed."

Hazel specialized in worst-case scenarios. Tuttle skipped down the stairs of his elevatorless building and got to his car just as a meter maid was beginning to write out a ticket. She was what was once described as a tomboy. She took off her uniform cap to reveal a crew cut. She scowled as Tuttle explained to her that he was an officer of the court on official business.

"What the hell does that mean?"

"I've got to run. Look. Go up to my office and talk to my secretary Hazel. She will explain."

"What's your name?"

Tuttle flashed an old police ID Peanuts had given him. "Hazel will explain."

He was in the car and behind the wheel now. He turned the key and the motor failed to start. Tuttle sent up a prayer to his father, tried again, and the motor coughed into life.

"Tuttle & Tuttle," he said to the meter maid. "Hazel will take care of everything."

If those two went mano a mano, Tuttle didn't know where he would lay his bet.

He pulled away from the curb and was nearly sideswiped by a passing car that followed its complaining horn down the street. Tuttle got into traffic and headed home for a restorative shower. You couldn't really be late for a funeral. It would run at least an hour, and it wasn't nine-thirty now.

As he drove he remembered the despair he had felt when he first got the news of Stanley Collins's death. One more golden opportunity receded from his grasp. He had bared his soul to the uncomprehending Peanuts, therapy of sorts, and then, later, at his desk, inspiration had come. And he had acted on it immediately. Sometimes he surprised himself. Somewhere his father was looking on benignly.

12

Shirley Escalante had been office manager for Sawyer and Collins for more than a year, hired after Mrs. Sawyer stopped working, and every other day she had thought of quitting. The place was a madhouse, largely because of the incessant civil war conducted by the two partners, each of whom tried to enlist her on his side in the struggle. It was hard to figure out what the quarreling was about. George did commercial property and Stanley domestic, and never the twain did meet. They were not competing with one another, the one's success was no skin off the nose of the other, but the bickering went on. Or backbiting. Most of it was conducted while the enemy was elsewhere and Shirley was the addressee of the latest grievance.

"He been in?" George Sawyer would say.

"I just spoke to him on the phone."

"Where was he calling from?"

"He didn't say."

"I'm not surprised."

A significant look. Shirley retained her neutrality. What was he getting at?

But the calls from Mrs. Collins were worse. Stanley always

signaled that he did not want to talk to her, and Shirley was reduced to telling lies no one would have believed.

"He just stepped out."

"Stepping out is what he does best."

What could she say? Even before she met Phyllis Collins there had been these veiled accusations against her husband. When Phyllis appeared in the office Shirley could scarcely believe her eyes. The photograph of her behind Stanley's desk was a studio portrait, delicately lighted, depicting a lovely woman with a dreamy look. In the flesh, Phyllis was something else entirely. She must have bought her clothes in the college coed section—everything that she wore was wrong. And her hair! Shirley had half a mind to give her a good shampoo and comb her hair out the way that it was in the studio portrait. Stiletto heels, miniskirt, that crazy hair—what was she trying to do?

"I'll wait in his office," she said, when it was clear that showing up unannounced had not enabled her to surprise her husband.

It was like a sit-in. Two hours she was in there, with the door closed, and when Stanley came in. Following a late lunch, Shirley was on the phone and didn't have a chance to warn him. He seemed puzzled that his door was shut, but he opened it and went in. Then all hell broke loose, she screeching, he yelling, it was awful. Shirley went down the hall to the ladies' and had a cigarette and then another, but they were still at it when she came back. But now George Sawyer stood outside the closed door, grinning at the battle going on in George's office.

"The wronged wife," he said, chuckling.

But Shirley's sympathy was with Stanley, and George Sawyer's attitude decided where she was on the war between the partners.

"This place is a madhouse," George said after five minutes and left.

Finally the door opened, and Mrs. Collins appeared. She

slammed the door shut behind her and glared at Shirley as if resenting her youth and good looks. She looked her up and down and was about to say something but then changed her mind. She couldn't have much voice left anyway after all that screaming.

Silence descended on the office after she was gone. Shirley kept glancing at the closed door of Stanley's office.

When he came out he was his unaltered self, smiling, breezy, devil-may-care. He said not a word about the family quarrel he must know she had heard. She admired him for his reticence, it was a classy way to handle it, and besides she was relieved that she did not have to respond to anything he might have said about his wife's visit.

"George isn't here?"

"He left."

He thought about that but didn't pursue it. Another point in his favor. If she could have thought of some acceptable way to do it, Shirley would have expressed her sympathy.

Such memories flooded her mind as she sat in a pew at St. Hilary's during the funeral Mass for her late employer. How long had it been since she had been to Mass? The grim reminder that Stanley had met the end that awaits us all, if not so violently, turned her mind to the religious faith that had shriveled and almost died. In the front pew, Phyllis Collins, all in black and, for a change, not dressed like a college girl, seemed to be weeping throughout the ceremony. The tall man in the pew behind her looked familiar, and then Shirley realized it was Dr. Jameson, the dentist to whom she owed her winsome smile. Throughout adolescence, Shirley had avoided smiling, not wanting to reveal the uneven teeth that gave her an almost Halloween look. She had seen a Jameson ad and resolved that she would have her teeth straightened, no matter that she was then twenty-two years old. She had gone ready to be told she must wear braces for years, with rubber binders holding it all together, and flash metal whenever she opened her mouth. She remembered kids like that. Jameson had laughed away her fears.

"No more, my dear. Not even your boyfriend will notice."

And he wouldn't have, if she had had one, but after Jameson had done his magic, Shirley's life was transformed. Men noticed her, women appraised her, she accepted every date she was offered. How absurd it all seemed. She was what she had always been but a few straightened teeth had changed everything. Beauty is only skin deep, and hers was by the skin of her teeth. She got her degree and landed the job with Sawyer and Collins and stopped responding to the attentions of random males. Shirley noticed that Bridget, Dr. Jameson's nurse, was in the church for the funeral of Stanley Collins.

George Sawyer was there, too, with his wife Susan, and there were a lot of old people, too. The priest who said the Mass and gave the sermon had a beautiful voice. Maybe, if she started practicing her religion again, Shirley would come here to St. Hilary's. It came as a surprise to find that Stanley was Catholic. Was George Sawyer too? Well, neither of them would have suspected that she was a cradle Catholic, so who was she to throw the first stone?

Outside, afterward, because of where she had parked, she found herself directed into the procession that was headed for the cemetery. She thought she could turn off along the way, but the chance never came. They were let through intersections with red lights and kept moving right along, so Shirley stayed with it.

At the cemetery, she did not get too close to those standing around the burial plot. In church, she had hardly noticed the coffin in which Stanley lay. Now it was inescapable that he would be lowered into the ground and earth piled over him. A little gasp escaped her, and she began to cry.

When things broke up, George Sawyer saw her, came and

touched her arm, and nodded. That was all. He seemed a little embarrassed by her teary eyes. As she went back to her car, a huge man caught up with her.

"I'm Lieutenant Horvath. I understand you worked for Stanley Collins."

"I'm the office manager of Sawyer-Collins."

"I wonder if we could have a little talk."

Good Lord, was it her smile? He seemed to read her mind.

"About Collins. I'm looking into the way he died. Just routine. But maybe you could help me."

"But why?"

"Someone killed him, didn't they?"

"He was hit by a car."

"That's what I mean. You busy now?"

What could she say? The office was closed for the day, out of respect. After what had happened to poor Mr. Collins, she had half a mind to leave the agency, but despite everything it was the best job she had ever had, and she had decided to stay on and see what it would be like without Stanley Collins there.

Tuttle had called Peanuts when he got out of the shower, and the two had gone to the funeral in a squad car. Peanuts said he would wait, so Tuttle went into the church alone. He was late, but that was all right. The sermon was just ending, and the rest was quick. Afterward, he wandered up and down the side aisle, against the grain of the departing congregation, showing the flag. He made sure Jameson saw him, and the widow, having convinced himself that they represented his ticket out of penury. He hung around on the steps outside, managing to catch the eye of the widow, and then went to the squad car and woke up Peanuts.

"How about the Great Wall? My treat."

Peanuts started the car, and they were off. The prospect of Chinese always galvanized Peanuts.

Later, with a table filled with exotic dishes, he told Peanuts all about Stanley's inheritance and the new plan to represent the widow. It was like talking aloud to himself, but not a waste of time, since it gave him a chance to put his thoughts in order.

The time he had spent studying the probated will of Frederick Collins had proved worthwhile. No wonder the man didn't kill himself selling real estate with the prospect of a bundle when he turned fifty. That still might be years away, but it was like knowing you were going to win the lottery. He had followed Collins around for a while before volunteering himself as counsel, trying to take the measure of the man. Collins's life seemed to consist of long lunches and many evenings on the town. The Rendezvous was a favorite and the singer there, Wanda Janski, was wonderful. Tuttle had kept out of eyesight of Collins, nursed a Dr Pepper, and wallowed in the sentimental ballads that brought back a youth Tuttle had never had. When Wanda sang "Smoke Gets In Your Eyes," Tuttle didn't mind the reek of liquor and clouds of cigarette smoke in the Rendezvous. Wanda's rendition of "You Belong to Me" made Tuttle glad for the dimness of the Rendezvous, no need to conceal the fact that he was bawling like a kid.

Tuttle's father had crooned these songs to his mother in the kitchen when the two of them did the dishes. He had sung them in the shower. He had hummed them in Mrs. Tuttle's ear and the two of them had snuggled like adolescents on the davenport while Tuttle beamed in approval. Had anyone had a happier childhood than he? Love songs stirred no personal romantic chord in Tuttle's heart; they brought back his parents and the house where there was love and not much else, since his father was only a letter carrier. Listening to Wanda was like being back in that crummy wonderful apartment on the south side with his father belting out one ballad after another. Those songs proved the entree to Stanley Collins.

"Haven't I seen you in the Rendezvous?" Tuttle said when he got past Shirley and into Collins's office.

"I don't know."

"Whatshername, Wanda. What a singer. I could listen to her all night."

"Lots of people do. What can I do for you?"

"I'm a lawyer. I came across your father's will down at the courthouse."

"What the hell did you do that for?"

"I just came upon it, in the course of research on another case. I hope you are drawing on the interest of the money your father gave you?"

"I don't get you."

So Tuttle had laid it out for him. Collins hadn't got a dime of his father's money yet, and Tuttle characterized that as damned near criminal.

"Amos Cadbury is a very shrewd lawyer, and I would wager he has made the principal grow dramatically."

For an alleged businessman, Stanley Collins was a babe in the woods. Had he thought his father's money was in a tin box, no more now than when he had left it for his son when he reached his fiftieth birthday? Apparently he had. And the prospect of tapping into it now was obviously welcome, plus the fact that he saw that he had been treated pretty shabbily by Amos Cadbury for nearly twenty years. Tuttle left the office as Collins's lawyer in the matter.

In a booth at the Rendezvous he told Collins of his visit to Amos Cadbury. Collins was devastated.

"So it can't be done."

"Of course it can be done. It will be done. You have my personal guarantee. Think of it. If Amos Cadbury had immediately fallen in with it, he would be, in effect, admitting that he had chiseled you. Now he will begin to consider the effects of that becoming known. A lawyer's reputation is his chief asset. This was just round one."

Wanda joined them after she had finished a set, and it was clear she and Collins were pretty close. Tuttle was shocked. Wanda was a knockout, even an old bachelor like Tuttle could appreciate that, but there was a Mrs. Collins, after all, and Tuttle associated the songs Wanda sang with marital fidelity and a loving couple doing dishes in the kitchen in an apartment on the south side.

There had been no occasion for a second visit to Amos Cadbury. Without warning, the grim reaper had come for Stanley Collins. So now it was on to Plan B, the widow, and Tuttle had an idea she would be even more eager than her late husband to get at that money.

"He was run over by his own car," Peanuts had told him. Then as now they were in a booth at the Great Wall.

"Come on."

Peanuts nodded. "It's true. They took it downtown."

"You're sure?"

"I'm telling you, ain't I?"

Tuttle stared at his ungifted friend. But Peanuts usually got things right when he reported to Tuttle about what was going on downtown.

"What's wrong?"

"Let's have another pot of tea."

Father Dowling was given a ride from the cemetery by Amos Cadbury. From behind tinted glass it took an act of faith to believe that the people he looked out at could not look in at him and Amos.

"In the case of the widow, it's just as well," Amos was saying. "I was there as a duty to the father rather than the son, may they both rest in peace."

"What of the widow?

"It is only partly confidential," Amos began, and on the drive to St. Hilary's he told Father Dowling of the widow's inquiry about her right to Stanley's inheritance.."Well, now she will get it all."

"When she is fifty?"

"No. That proviso lapses with the death of Stanley."

"So she is a wealthy woman?"

"She will be very comfortable," Amos said. "If such a person is ever comfortable."

"Have you told her?"

"Oh, no. I am under no obligation to rush to her with such venal news." He began unwrapping a cigar with great concentration. "Indeed, I shall proceed with deliberate speed to tell her. Much as it will ease the grief of her loss."

Father Dowling had never heard Amos so censorious, however obliquely. But then he himself had met Phyllis Collins and was able to appreciate Amos's judgment of the woman.

"She might have lost it all," Amos said, after lighting his cigar with all deliberate speed.

"How so?"

"If Stanley had divorced her when he was not in possession of the inheritance, it could hardly figure in any settlement."

"Not even if it were coming to him when he was fifty?"

"Any lawyer could have sequestered the money from the settlement." He let cigar smoke slide from between his lips, smiling. "Even your friend Tuttle."

"My friend?"

"You like everyone, Father Dowling. All us sinners."

"Just like attracting like."

"Ho, ho."

"It's been a while since I've seen Tuttle."

"I cannot say the same."

The visit from Tuttle as Stanley's putative legal representative was recalled by Amos with something approaching relish.

"He may have no difficulty wishing to break a will, but he could scarcely enlist me to break a will I myself had made."

So each of the Collinses had approached Amos about the inheritance, only to be disappointed, Phyllis perhaps most of all. Whether it was Stanley who divorced her, or she who divorced Stanley—Father Dowling still had not decided which of the aggrieved spouses had told him the truth when they had visited him separately at the rectory—Phyllis would thereby be cut off from the fortune awaiting Stanley when he turned fifty.

"One might say that Phyllis Collins is the great beneficiary of the unhappy accident that made her a widow."

"Accident?" Amos's eyebrows rose expressively.

"I suppose a hit-and-run involves some element of intention."

"Haven't you heard that it was Stanley's own car that ran him down?"

"But who would have been driving?"

After a long silence, Amos said, "It could be that the widow might not inherit after all."

They fell silent as the great car purred along on the way to the St. Hilary's rectory. Had Phyllis Collins come away from her meeting with Amos Cadbury with a motive to end her marriage in a manner that would not cut her off from her husband's inheritance?

"Did you tell her what might happen in the event of Stanley's death?"

"Certainly not. But it is something that could easily have been ascertained. Perhaps by her apparent protector, David Jameson."

Amos was in a rare mood, no doubt of that. Here was an almost catty side to the distinguished lawyer that Father Dowling would not have suspected. And then his motive became clear.

"I myself would hardly be the one to bring such matters to the attention of the police, Father Dowling. Assuming that they deserve attention. But you must admit that learning it was Stanley's own car that ran him down does set the mind going."

"You must come in," Father Dowling said, when they arrived at the rectory.

"Thank you, no, Father. But give my regards to Mrs. Murkin."

Watching the large black car with tinted windows drive away, Father Dowling had the impression that Amos had accomplished what he had set out to when he offered him a ride from the cemetery.

* * *

The following day, Father Dowling passed on to Phil Keegan the burden of Amos Cadbury's communication. He devoted some thought to it before doing so. What he was providing was a motive for Phyllis Collins to kill her husband, but it was a long stretch from that motive to the opportunity and execution of any such desire, and Father Dowling, of course, had no idea whether Phyllis Collins could have used her husband's car as a murder weapon and then returned it to the parking lot of the Rendezvous.

"Returned it?" Phil said. "Who says it was there?"

"I thought Stanley had been in the Rendezvous."

"So why was he walking down the street? Where the body was found does not suggest that he was on the way to the parking lot. That was in the opposite direction."

"Why indeed?"

"To find a cab? To hoof it to the apartment of Wanda Janski?"

It appeared that not only his car keys were found on Stanley but house keys as well, not all of them to the house he shared with Phyllis. He now brought the pastor of St. Hilary's up to speed on what had been learned in the past twenty-four hours.

The scarf found on the front seat of Stanley's car was his wife's, and she had no explanation of why it happened to be there.

"No big deal," Phil conceded. "She might have left it there at any time."

"Is that what she said?"

"There was no need to. She was happy to have it back when Agnes Lamb gave it to her." Phil sighed. "Well, now the poor devil is safely underground."

But the mystery of Stanley's death had not been buried with him, and Father Dowling was sure that the police would pursue the matter.

"I suppose the wife had a set of keys to the car?"

Phil smiled. "I suppose."

After Phil left, Father Dowling sat in his study. It was here that he had spoken with Stanley and later with his wife. His proposal that they come together to see him had not been acted on. Their troubled marriage had been terminated in a way neither must have foreseen when they came to him. Now Phyllis Collins, the woman who dressed like a girl, had come into the wealth she coveted. Did that mean that the way had been smoothed for David Jameson?

After the funeral David Jameson came back to the house with her, George Sawyer, and his wife Susan as well. It was nice of them, and Phyllis would not have wanted to be left alone. She had spent sleepless nights since the terrible news of Stanley's death was brought to her last Friday morning by one of the policemen who had found the body. How had she gotten through that unreal encounter?

She had been watching television, something she had been doing a lot of since Stanley had begun to spend entire nights at Wanda Janski's apartment, a studio on the top floor of a building not two blocks from the agency. From the street, you could see the lights of the apartment, as Phyllis had discovered when she began to spy on her husband. She had parked several doors away and tried to make herself as small as possible. What would anyone who noticed make of a woman just sitting in a parked car at night on a deserted street? Ten minutes after she parked, she had told herself that this was stupid and demeaning. What need did she have of proof that Stanley saw other women? That was something she had known for years, and Stanley had known she had known and didn't care. He expected her not to care either.

"Phyl, it's not important."

"Not important!"

"It's the way of the world, for God's sake. I didn't invent it. You know I love you."

"Love me? What does that mean?"

"That you can raise hell with me about this, go ahead, but when all is said and done, you're my wife and I'm your husband."

"You're a monster."

"A tired monster, then. And a little drunk."

And he had gone off to bed. She would have expected him to deny it or pretend he was sorry, anything but that casual sloughing it off as if it really didn't matter.

She should have left him then. If she had any pride at all, she would have. But even to think the thought had filled her with terror. What would she do? The job she'd had before they were married had bored her to tears, and it had hardly paid enough to keep her when she was single. She could not stand the thought of being on her own again. It would not have been the same thing anyway. She would have been a wronged wife, abandoned. And, of course, there was that constant point of reference of their marriage, the money Stanley would come into when he turned fifty. Once she had worried that Susan Sawyer might become an object of Stanley's insatiable appetite. Now, that would have seemed like keeping it in the firm.

What a cruel provision in his father's will that had been. To leave him money and then not let him get at it until he was middle-aged. The worst part was that Stanley accepted it. He seemed to like the thought of postponed prosperity. God knows he wasn't much at real estate. George Sawyer had several times threatened to end their partnership, his point being that he was carrying Stanley. In any case, the insurance the two partners carried on one another was an expensive bond between them. Whenever they had that argument, Stanley would become a whirlwind and sell half a dozen houses and be on top of the world. But it never lasted. It was as if he already had a fortune and needed only to wait for it.

"There must be a way to get it sooner."

"I doubt it. Twice I put it as a hypothetical case to old Hoover who used to do work for the agency. He showed interest until I told him who had drawn up the will. Amos Cadbury? Hoover just shook his head. Not even dynamite could break a will Amos Cadbury had written."

"Then go to Cadbury."

"And beg?"

"How can you beg for what is yours?"

Their marriage had been like that. Not marrying in the Church was the beginning. Phyllis's mother was devastated. She did not come to the civil ceremony. No one did. The witnesses were strangers pressed into service on the spur of the moment. The idea was that it was kind of a trial marriage. Later they would have it blessed and everything would be all right. But that meant that in the meantime they really weren't married. It occurred to Phyllis that this was an escape hatch for Stanley. She hadn't wanted time to be sure she wanted to marry him. It was hard to believe, sometimes, how much in love with him she had been. So much in love that she had agreed to his suggestion that they begin with a civil marriage.

"I talked with a priest and he suggested it."

"A priest?"

"People get married in the Church and then that's it. But a civil marriage is different."

"Don't you want to be really married?"

He took her in his arms. "What difference does the kind of ceremony make?"

He knew as well as she did; he had been raised Catholic, too. After their marriage, they had not gone to church. From the Church's point of view they were living in sin. That thought bothered Phyllis more than she would have expected. More and more as time went on. What were they waiting for? She began to fear that Stanley was waiting until he found an interesting replacement for her. But the women he went out with were not women he would likely marry. Certainly not Wanda Janski. But Phyllis had come to doubt this.

He would meet women in bars, or they were divorcées who were setting up on their own and wanted to rent an apartment. Stanley must have looked pretty attractive to someone suddenly on her own and a little frightened by the thought. They were vulnerable and Stanley took advantage. The first one Phyllis found out about was a client of Stanley's. But Wanda had become almost permanent.

And then, at last, she had come to know David Jameson. It was pleasant having him so attentive and respectful; he never really tried anything, but then he was shy. Phyllis had the feeling she could easily lead him on into a more serious relationship. Talking with him about her problems was already a species of infidelity. How encouraging it was to have him take her side without question. When he heard about the inheritance, listening in silent attention, he took her by the arms.

"I wondered how he managed to keep you."

"What do you mean?"

"It's a bribe, don't you see? He talked you into thinking that the point of your life would be reached on his fiftieth birthday."

"David, I am not mercenary."

"That money is as much yours as it is his. Given his behavior, I think you would be unwise to wait."

"What do you mean?"

"Phyllis, he could divorce you. Can't you see that was the whole point of a civil marriage? I wouldn't be surprised if he intends to drop you a year or so before he comes into that money."

Phyllis protested, trying to come to Stanley's defense, but she could not dispel the thought that Stanley eventually meant to end their marriage.

"That would leave you out in the cold."

He spelled it out for her. The inheritance would probably not figure in any divorce settlement. Phyllis might share in what they now had.

"That isn't much."

"And he could marry another woman in the Church."

"No!"

David nodded. He knew all about such things. He had read canon law and everything. The thought of Stanley before the altar with another woman was the turning point. She agreed with David that she would have to act before Stanley did. So they had gone to see Amos Cadbury. With crushing results. Now she had it from Amos Cadbury himself that a divorce would cut her off from that damnable inheritance. She could not have borne the disappointment without David's consolation. And that was when she suggested that they should go to bed together, not that she had put it that boldly. He had not responded with a sermon as she feared he would.

"Why did you never marry?"

He looked at her tenderly.

"I was waiting for the right woman."

*　*　*

Susan was not shy to say what she thought of David's coming to the house after the funeral.

"What's he doing here?" Susan asked when they were alone. David was having a drink with George in the living room.

"He's my dentist."

Susan tucked in her chin.

"Our dentist. And a good friend."

But Susan's manner was not accusative. "I don't blame you."

Phyllis was angered by the assumption that she had a man ready to take Stanley's place, which was clearly what Susan thought. After the wake and the funeral, she felt differently toward David than she had. And it occurred to her that she was now Stanley's uncontested heir.

"I should have asked Bob to come back here," she said to Susan.

"Bob?"

"My brother."

"I didn't know you had a brother."

So she told Susan about her brother the journalist. "You must have seen his features in the *Tribune*. Bob Oliver. I suggested to him once that he do a feature on the agency."

"What did he say?"

"He wasn't interested."

"Is that all?"

"What do you mean?"

Susan studied her for a moment, as if looking for something in her manner. "He just forgot all about it?"

"I guess. It never came up again. He must not have thought it was such a great idea."

"I'm sure he was right about that."

* * *

Bob showed up at the house after the Sawyers had left, taking Phyllis in his arms. It had been years since the thought of having a brother seemed a plus to her. She told Bob of Susan's surprise that she had a brother.

"I must be forgettable."

"Oh, she knew who you were when I described you."

"Good for her."

"Do you know her?"

"That would be telling."

Men. She could have kicked him. But then he took her in his arms again, and she pressed against him.

The keys to his car were among the things found on the body of Stanley Collins, something Cy Horvath could not forget. Whoever had run over Stanley had another key to his car. But no ignition key had been found in Stanley's car. Of course, whoever had used the car as a murder weapon, if that was what happened, could have pitched the keys into any Dumpster in town or tossed them into the Fox River. It was the fact that the car had been found where, apparently, Stanley had left it, in the parking lot of the Rendezvous, that set Cy's mind in motion.

When he spoke with Shirley Escalante at the cemetery she

had not found his question surprising. Yes, there was a set of Stanley's car keys at the office.

"I keep extra keys for both of them, house keys, car keys. I even have the key to George Sawyer's personal safe-deposit box."

"Can we check to see if they are still there?"

They weren't. She had keys all over her desk, but the keys to Stanley's car were not among them.

"He must have taken them without telling me."

Cy did not comment. He thanked her and went on to the Rendezvous.

"Who works nights, Joe?" he asked Perzel.

"There are three bartenders at night and a platoon of waitresses. That's the money time of day for the bar. Wanda is a big attraction."

"The woman who showed up at the wake?"

Joe nodded, a silly smile on his face. Well, maybe Wanda looked good in the dim lights of the Rendezvous. Cy brought Marge along when he checked the place out.

"The Rendezvous?"

"You've heard of it?"

"Cy, everyone has heard of it."

Except Lieutenant Horvath, apparently. Cy went to bed early unless something he was working on dictated otherwise. Marge was glad enough to have a few drinks in the dimly lit bistro, ordering a daiquiri and lighting up a cigarette while they waited for their drinks to come. Cy had ordered beer and Marge made a face when he did.

"What's a daiquiri?"

"Oh, Cy."

He felt he was out with a stranger, not his wife. And then Wanda began to sing, leaning against the piano and seeming to make love to the microphone she held. Conversation died. All eyes were on her. She did look good in the lights of the bar, but she could have been ugly with a voice like that. The songs she sang made Marge's eyes misty, as if the singer were recalling the youth of everyone in the room. Cy had no ear for music, which may have been why he screened out what passed for popular music nowadays, but the lyrics of the ballads Wanda Janski sang figured in the biography of everyone listening to her. She drifted from one song into the next, stilling the applause that began, that could wait until she was done. For now, she was wholly absorbed in the plaintive lyrics she half whispered, half sang, into the smoky air of the Rendezvous. Marge reached out and took his hand.

"Remember?"

Cy remembered. "To Each His Own." "Sentimental Journey." "That's My Desire." It was the repertoire of youth, of early love, of music when it had spoken to the heart instead of the loins. The "Chatanooga Choo Choo" altered the mood, followed by "Chicago, My Kind of Town," but then Wanda sang "You Belong to Me" and Marge kept squeezing Cy's hand. He squeezed back. Joe Perzel had said that Stanley and Wanda had been an item, but every man in the room was in love with her, so what did it mean?

Wanda disappeared when she finished her set, and the noise level rose. Cy left Marge with her daiquiri and teary eyes and went to have a talk with Basil the bartender.

"Hey, I'm busy, okay?"

Cy showed him his identification. "It's about Stanley Collins."

"Geez."

But Basil left the bar to his acolytes and led Cy down a narrow hallway to a room where the help took its breaks.

"Can we make it quick?"

"We could talk tomorrow morning."

"Mornings I sleep."

"You knew Stanley Collins?"

Basil was fat in a way that made thin seem an offense. His face was damp with perspiration, but he was the kind of man who would have sweated at the North Pole. A heart attack waiting to happen. Cy thought of Stanley lying on the slab at the morgue as Pippin went about her work.

Basil had known Stanley. He was a regular.

"Look, the one you should talk to is Wanda."

"She disappeared."

"Her dressing room's next door."

Cy stood. "I'll get back to you."

Basil was scurrying down the hallway to the bar when Cy rapped on the door of Wanda's dressing room. No answer, so he knocked harder, and tried the knob. It turned and the door opened.

Wanda sat at a dressing table, a drink before her, studying her face in the mirror. She looked at Cy in the mirror.

"Who are you?"

"Lieutenant Horvath."

"You were at the wake."

"So were you. Can we talk?"

"I go on again in ten minutes."

"You're good."

She turned. Once she would have been beautiful. In a way, she still was. But what had once been curves had turned into flesh. Her hair was startling in its amplitude.

"I like blondes no matter what color their hair is."

"This is my natural color. At least it was."

"Tell me about Stanley."

She laughed. "Just like that."

"At first it seemed just a hit-and-run. Only the car that ran him down was his own. It was found in the parking lot here. Mysterious."

"It could have been anyone."

"He had that many enemies?"

"I don't think he had any."

"How well did you know him?"

"Well enough that he asked me to marry him."

"He was already married."

"That was over."

"Everything is over now."

She began to cry. Not dramatically, not making a thing of it, just crying. "I never really counted on it. I'm a big girl now, beyond dreaming wild dreams. All my dreams are tied up with the lyrics of old songs. You have to be a certain age to appreciate them."

Cy nodded. "My wife got all teared up."

"I know. People do. They affect me the same way. There were generations of people who let songs think for them, and it wasn't all that bad. Did you ever listen to a *rapper?*"

"Not on purpose."

"It started with rock. Everything but feeling. Jazz gets to some people, but most of them are like wine snobs. My kind of music speaks the truth to most people. At least it did."

"Stanley," he reminded her.

"I don't know. I thought they were kidding when they told me. He had been here that night."

"Hence his car in the parking lot. What was he doing on the street, waiting to get run over?"

"He was probably drunk. He liked to get drunk. Nice drunk, mellow, out of himself."

"Did you know he had left?"

"You've been out there. How much do you suppose I see of the people I sing to? I don't even try. I sing to myself as much as anything."

"It wasn't an accident, Wanda."

"If you say so."

"He must have had enemies."

"Well, he had a partner."

"George Sawyer?"

"Talk to him."

"Everyone tells me to talk to somebody else."

"Lieutenant, if I could help you, I would. When Stanley died, the last candle on my cake went out. As I said, I wasn't surprised. But even so, it might have happened. We might have married . . ."

Her voice trailed away. It might have been a line from a lyric.

Marge had another daiquiri and Cy ordered another beer. He could have got a six-pack for what he was paying for it.

"We ought to do this more often, Cy."

"I can't afford it."

"Next time I'll order beer, too."

"Don't. It costs more than your mouthwash."

A little stir as the light picked up Wanda, back at the piano, smiling into the lights, and then she began again. There are stations in major cities around the nation that specialize in golden oldies, which was how Wanda's repertoire would have been categorized. Cy doubted that the hits of the present day would elicit this kind of reaction in any imaginable future. She sang "Lazy River," "Ain't Misbehavin'," "I Gotta Right to Sing the Blues," melding them as before, lest the mood be spoiled by applause. A few lively numbers and then her finale, which Cy would learn was her signature song, a theft from Frankie, "My Way."

"What was she like?" Marge asked in the car.

"About a C cup."

"Cy."

"There's a lot to her."

"You like big women."

"Only when they squeeze my hand."

She put her head on his shoulder and hummed all the way home.

Those who thought they knew Marie Murkin might have imagined quite a different reaction to that with which she met the visitor at the rectory that afternoon. But it was the visitor who was uncomfortable, not Marie.

"You don't remember me," the woman said.

"Help me."

"My mother was Marian Janski."

"The organist!"

"I'm Wanda."

Marie took her right into the front parlor, anxious to put together the reference to the parish organist of long ago and this highly made-up woman who looked, in the phrase, as if she had been around the block.

"Did you move away?" Marie asked.

"Out of the parish? Yes." But her tone suggested a more decisive removal. Marie had objected to Phyllis Collins's excessive makeup but had no trouble with Wanda's. Not after she decided she was an artist.

"Your whole family was musical, Wanda."

"There was only my brother Gerry and myself."

"And your mother. What an organist!" Marie brought her hands together and threw back her head. Then she looked at Wanda. "Not that the Franciscans appreciated her."

"Mom loved playing that organ. But then arthritis put a stop to it."

Marie shook her head. "Why is that the good suffer so?" The remark brought tears to Wanda's eyes.

"She was a good woman."

"The best."

Having canonized the late Marian Janski, the stage was set for discovering what had brought Wanda to the rectory. To block one possible avenue, Marie made a point of saying how committed they were to Mrs. Sharp, the current organist, even though she couldn't hold a candle to Wanda's mother.

"I play piano and sing for a living."

"You do. Tell me about it."

"In a nightclub. I like it well enough, I guess. But what's the point, really?"

"You never married?"

The eyes, heavy with mascara, did not meet Marie's. And then Father Dowling stood in the parlor door.

"I thought I heard voices."

Marie jumped up. "Father, this is Wanda Janski. Her mother was the parish organist, before your time."

"And you've come to see Marie."

"I had hoped to see you."

"Any objection, Marie?"

Marie avoided looking at Wanda. That was as close to scolding as Father Dowling ever got.

"I couldn't resist talking about old times," Marie said.

"Of course not."

He let her go back to the kitchen before he turned to Wanda.

Talking with Marie had helped, but Wanda was visibly uneasy when she was alone with Father Dowling.

"I feel like a phony, talking about my mother like that. Father, I haven't been to church in years."

"I'm sorry to hear that."

"It was mainly my job at first. Entertainment doesn't give you a chance to lead a regular life. I traveled with a group for a couple years and then did this and that and ended up singing in clubs, but it's all night work and when morning comes you're out like a light."

"Including Sunday morning?"

She nodded.

"I suppose that's one reason we have the Saturday evening Mass."

Wanda didn't know about that. So she had been away a long time. Most of her adult life as it turned out.

"I'm forty-seven."

"Not many women mention their age."

"Not many have to."

He smiled. "Never married?"

There was a long silence. "Can this count as confession, Father?"

In answer, he closed the door and took a stole from a drawer of the desk.

"I suppose it's been a while since you did this."

"A lifetime. But do you know, I still remember the formula the sisters taught us." She closed her eyes. "Bless me, Father, for I have sinned. My last confession was . . ." She opened her eyes. "I don't remember. I do remember my first confession, though. I was so eager to tell the priest all my imaginary sins."

"Imaginary?"

"They seem so now," she said wistfully. "Why do we have to grow up?"

"Most of us just grow older rather than up."

"Father, I've committed just about every sin there is."

She was an improbable Magdalene, with her mountain of blonde hair, the make-up, what he imagined was a very expensive dress, but the distress in her eyes was unmistakable. He helped her examine her conscience. She was in a mood to admit to every capital sin; he suspected she would confess to murder if he asked her.

"You said you never married," he said, easing into that department.

"No. But I might have. There was a man . . ."

He was about to cut her off. He didn't want her waxing nostalgic about her past, but she went on.

"He was married, so there was that, too, adultery. And not for the first time. But he was going to get a divorce and then we would marry." She looked at him pathetically. "That sounds like a line, doesn't it? But he meant it, I know he did."

132   Ralph McInerny

"What happened?"

"He's dead."

Perhaps the dashing of her dream explained as much as anything her coming to the rectory. What courage that must have taken. Again he was grateful that Marie had waylaid Wanda and put her at ease. Would she have been able to do this if she hadn't talked about her mother with Marie?

"He was Catholic, at least he had been, but he hadn't been married in the Church. He told me we could have a real wedding when we married, in the Church, the whole thing. The way you dream of it when you're a kid. Not that I would have worn white."

"But he died?"

"He was killed."

Of course, he could not ask her the man's name. He realized he didn't have to. Wanda was the woman Phyllis had come to complain about. Where this certitude came from it would have been difficult to say. And then she said he had been struck by a car.

"I think I read about that."

"Then you read my obituary, too."

He got her back to her sins and when he gave her absolution her expression had softened.

"Is that it?"

"That's it. Your sins are forgiven."

"It was easy."

"Don't let so much time go by before next time. And look into that Saturday afternoon Mass. It counts for Sunday."

"Do you have one here?"

He nodded. "Five o'clock."

"My mother did play the organ here."

"So I guess St. Hilary's is your parish."

"He said we would get married here."

Father Dowling let it go.

After she was gone, he went down the hall to the kitchen.

"Don't come in. I just scrubbed the floor."

"As a penance?"

But Marie was beyond any sheepishness she had felt about detouring Wanda by the front parlor.

Gerry Janksi was an accountant at the *Fox River Tribune*, specializing in the swindle sheets of reporters who were always trying to supplement their salaries with inflated expense claims. But Gerry insisted on receipts. Not that he didn't sometimes accept collateral evidence of expenditures. Bob Oliver just could not acquire the habit of keeping receipts, but his stories made it easy to reconstruct what he had spent in the line of duty. Bob was nuts about Sylvia Woods, the photographer he always insisted on for his stories, but Sylvia was Gerry's girl, their little secret.

"Why can't I tell him, Gerry? It would get him off my back."

"I told you my goal."

Gerry had been saving and investing. He intended to retire when he married and take Sylvia to Florida and never add another column of figures for the rest of his life. Meanwhile, they would remain secretly engaged.

"We're both getting old."

Sylvia was thirty, twelve years younger than Gerry, but she could have been twenty. All he had to do to placate her was tell her what a great wedding they would have, at St. Hilary's where he had grown up.

"You still a parishioner?"

"That doesn't matter anymore."

"You still practice?"

For a minute he thought she meant the violin. He had kept the damned thing until a few years ago. Now all he played was the mouth organ, a far more versatile instrument than he would have believed. And you could carry it around in your pocket. On dates, he would sometimes play it for Sylvia, and she was enthralled. Apparently she did not realize that Wanda was his sister, the toast of the town, at least some of the town. It broke Gerry's heart to think of Wanda singing at the Rendezvous. But if that was bad, her running around with a married man, Stanley Collins, was worse. She should be playing the organ in church like their mother.

"I go to Mass, of course," Gerry said in answer to Sylvia's question.

She smiled. "I like that 'of course.'"

"It's the way I was raised."

"Me, too."

His was a staid life while Wanda's seemed to be the kind they had been warned about by the nuns. The primrose path of dalliance. The sweet siren song of the world leading you farther and farther from God. The funny thing was that Wanda agreed with him when he told her this.

"Gerry, it's not what you think."

"What do I think?"

"You know. But when we marry . . ."

"He's already got a wife."

"They weren't married in the Church. It wasn't a real wedding."

"Come on."

·

"Ask anyone. A civil marriage, not a sacramental marriage."

"Did he explain all this to you?"

"Gerry, don't be so hard on me. If we marry in the Church everything will be all right."

"If."

Her face fell, as if she found it as improbable as he did. Stanley Collins, Gerry had learned, was a real Romeo. Wanda was just the latest girl on his list. Had he told them all he really wasn't married? Gerry did not believe for a minute that Stanley Collins intended to marry Wanda. Neither did Willie Boiardo.

"The guy's in real estate. He's a stranger to honesty."

Boiardo wasn't in the phone book, but Gerry had learned where he lived by calling the manager of the Rendezvous, claiming he was a fellow musician anxious to see old Willie. He could have said he was Wanda's brother and would have if the first excuse hadn't worked, but he was told Willie had a room at the Frosinone. The Frosinone! When Bob Oliver had mentioned doing a story on local architecture that would feature the Frosinone, Gerry had kept quiet. Bob was no idiot, and one visit to the Frosinone would be enough for him to figure it out.

"It's part of the Pianone operation," he told Sylvia.

"A hotel?"

"They have women who work out of there. They call them escorts." He showed her the full-page ad in the Yellow Pages.

"You mean they're . . ."

Gerry nodded. Sylvia laughed. "It was the run-down condition of the place that turned Bob off."

Telling Sylvia about the Frosinone stirred Gerry's curiosity about the hotel. Who was the British prime minister who had cruised London at night, talking with streetwalkers, telling himself he wanted to help them extricate themselves from their fallen lives? Gerry felt a bit like that the afternoon after work when he strolled from the *Tribune* to the Frosinone and went inside. He had half expected the bar to be teeming with available escorts but it was deserted except for a little guy who had to be Willie Boiardo.

"I'm Gerry Janski."

Willie squinted at him, tipped his head to one side, then nodded. "Sure. I see the resemblance. Pull up a pew."

He listened to the long sad story of Willie's life, told with such evident pleasure it was hard to tell whether the pianist saw it as tragedy or comedy. He noticed Gerry's confusion.

"You're still young enough to think that there is a lot of difference between success and failure. They're not the same, granted. But they're both temporary. Know what I mean? You'll never get out of this world alive."

"Isn't that a song?"

"Country western. How come I never met you before?"

"I work for a living."

A barking little laugh. "Wanda said all her family is musical."

Gerry displayed his harmonica.

"Play something."

Gerry played "On Top of Old Smoky," "Beautiful Brown Eyes," "Lavender's Blue," and "He's Got the Whole World in His Hands." People began to come into the bar while he played but it was Willie's response that gratified Gerry. Willie led the applause when Gerry had finished.

"I wouldn't have believed you could get all that out of a mouth organ."

Several girls had come into the bar and one came sailing over to their table.

"Hi. I'm Flora. That was wonderful."

She was joined by a swarthy frowning man who might have been her father. It was Primo Verdi, the manager. Gerry thanked Flora, and Verdi led her away.

"He should put a chastity belt on her," Willie said.

"Is he her father?"

"He used to be her husband."

"Used to be?"

"It's a long story, and I'd rather tell you mine."

"How long have you been with Wanda?"

Gerry had a pretty good idea of the answer to that, but he wanted to get Willie talking about Wanda. And Stanley Collins. That was when he learned Willie's estimate of the Realtor who had taken up so much of Wanda's time.

"She thinks he's going to marry her."

"Over my dead body." But his expression softened. "Gerry, without Wanda I'm through."

Edna Hospers had lived in St. Hilary parish ever since she married Earl, and after he ran afoul of the law and was sent to Joliet, she had stayed on with the kids. She might have left, out of shame, if Father Dowling had not suggested she turn the parish school into a meeting place for older parishioners. The effort had prospered and now there was a solid group of daily regulars as well as less frequent oldsters. Edna kept it simple, not wanting to make things too busy. People were content to play cards, talk, and, from time to time, go on one of the shuttle runs to a mall. Edna wanted it to be a place where old people could just relax and do what old people do, which seemed for the most part to be talking about their grandchildren.

Given the age difference, Edna hadn't known the parish seniors before she got to know them in her capacity as director of the center. Of late, conversation had turned on what had happened to Stanley, the son of the Collinses.

"He was a late baby," Mrs. Maguire said.

"Now he's a late man." Charley Schwartz was the wit of the group that played hearts every day. Edna was sitting in for the absent Peggy Wilson.

"What a thing to say."

"How would you put it?"

"I wouldn't. Deal."

Hands were distributed and silence reigned. They played a serious game. After five minutes, Mrs. Maguire, triumphant, was prepared to be more indulgent to Charley Schwartz.

"I had my last baby when I was thirty-one."

"Well, don't look at me," Charley Schwartz said.

She didn't. "Jessica Collins must have been nearly forty when she had Stanley,"

"Thirty-seven," said Molly Berg.

"You're sure?"

"I was working in Maternity when he was born. In those days, that was considered a late birth, and special care was taken. Now grandmothers have children."

"Grandchildren?" Schwartz asked.

"Not this grandmother," Mrs. Maguire said. "I've done my bit."

"You had seven?"

"That lived."

Charley grew restive. Widows outnumbered widowers two to

one at the center, but he didn't want a lot of woman talk. "Let's play cards."

"Are you thinking of learning how?"

"Ouch."

After another hand, Edna excused herself and went upstairs to her office, once the principal's suite. It was there that Father Dowling found her half an hour later.

"How's Earl doing?"

"He's got a job! With UPS. Father, we can't begin to tell you . . ."

He stopped her, as she knew he would. Of course, she had told him again and again how grateful she was, how grateful they all were, for what he had done that had brought Earl once more back home. It had been difficult at first. However much the children liked having a father in the house, after years of having a single parent it was hard for them to act naturally. And Earl had been restless while he interviewed at various places. His background was not an asset, but, of course, he had to mention it. The parole officer helped, but his help only underscored the fact that Earl had spent years at Joliet, and for manslaughter.

There had been times when Edna had been really angry with Earl for taking responsibility for Sylvia Lowry's death. But she had come to understand the way he thought of it. It was the same stubbornness that made him be front and center with his conviction, and the fact that he was on parole. There were some who could admire his conscientiousness, and Edna despite herself was one of them, but not many potential employers were eager to have an ex-convict on their payroll. Finally he had found a job, and one just suited to him.

"If only I didn't have to wear this damned uniform."

"Earl, it doesn't look like a uniform."

"Doesn't it? It feels like one."

The uniformed guards at Joliet were the enemy, of course, and

Earl had adopted the common attitude toward them. But all that was past now, thank God, and they would never forget Father Dowling's role in Earl's release.

"Earl will do fine."

"I know." She had been fiercely loyal to him during the awful years of his absence, and she was not likely to change now that he was free.

"Is there much talk among the old people about what happened to Stanley Collins?"

"Many of them knew his parents."

"Strange case. Apparently it wasn't a hit-and-run."

Captain Keegan was a good friend of the pastor's and now that Earl was home Edna was prepared to think differently about him. For years she had resented the fact that the police hadn't dismissed Earl's confession and saved him from himself, but she knew that was foolish.

"He left a lot of money to his son, but it was being held back until he was fifty."

"Fifty!"

"His father didn't think Stanley would be grown up until then, I guess."

"And now he'll never get it."

"But someone will."

"His widow."

"She is a great favorite of David Jameson."

Edna made a face. "Do you know he asked me if he could spend time here, be a sort of counselor to the old people? He said it was to try his vocation."

"And what did you tell him?"

"That you were all the counselor they need. What's wrong with him?"

"He thinks he should have been a priest."

"What religion?"

Father Dowling laughed.

"Shame on me, Father. I've been playing cards at a table with Charley Schwartz."

"Good old Charley."

"You should hear him on Jameson."

"Oh."

"Jameson told him he needed a root canal and Charley said he would get a second opinion before undergoing anything that serious. The other dentist told him it wasn't necessary. Now whenever Jameson is mentioned, he goes, 'Quack, quack.'"

"Maybe the second dentist was wrong."

"He pulled out all Charley's teeth and sold him a new set."

"Did he get a second opinion before doing that?"

"I didn't ask."

"Dr. Jameson is no quack, I'm sure of that."

"Bridget certainly thinks the world of him. If I ever relent and let him work on me it will be for her sake."

Tuttle let a decent interval go by after the funeral before he called on Phyllis Collins—twenty-four hours. For a while it looked like she wouldn't let him in, and they spoke through the screen door, but Tuttle was inured to disdain.

"That was great advice you gave about going to Amos Cadbury.

I was never so embarrassed in my life." So Stanley had told her of that.

"Well, everything has changed now."

Through the mesh of the screen she looked the way photographs in the newspaper once had looked, an arrangement of dots. She undid the hook and opened the door. Tuttle swept off his tweed hat as he entered but put it on again when he was inside.

"What has changed?"

But the way she asked, he figured she already knew. "You are your husband's heir."

"I don't think he had a will."

"It doesn't matter. By state law, you get everything."

"All his debts."

"Was he in debt?"

"That's what his partner, George Sawyer, tells me."

Tuttle frowned. "How much?"

"God only knows."

Tuttle ran a stubby finger along the brim of his cap. "Whatever it is, you can afford it. But we'll have to drive a hard bargain with Sawyer."

She accepted the "we" and Tuttle grew bolder.

"I want your authorization to consult with Amos Cadbury. He is the trustee, but with the death of Stanley, the proviso of waiting until his fiftieth birthday is moot."

"'Moot'?"

"Mrs. Collins, he will never see fifty now."

She gave a little cry. Well, after all, she was a widow, no matter how choppy her marriage had been.

"How did you learn about the will in the first place?"

Tuttle considered before he answered. He might have chalked

it up to simple legal curiosity, but complete candor did not seem called for.

"Your brother, Bob."

"Oh, my God. I told him about it in a weak moment. He had heard about Stanley's playing around and told me I should divorce the sonofabitch."

It seemed a direct quote. And Tuttle could imagine Bob Oliver saying it. Bob had been in real estate himself, in a small way, handling properties that went on the market for failure to pay taxes and then selling them to young couples as opportunities for restoration. He had made a career out of envying Stanley until he switched to journalism.

Tuttle had said to him, "He's not as prosperous as you think, Bob." Tuttle had asked around. He already knew about George Sawyer's grousing about his partner:

"The sonofabitch will come into a fortune when he's fifty."

Tuttle had heard enough stories of this kind to be skeptical, but he had checked it out and found that Bob was right. He took Bob to show him the will. So Tuttle approached Stanley and got his okay to see what he could do with Amos Cadbury. And Stanley had told his wife, probably playing it as a trump during a domestic quarrel. She had checked with Tuttle and that had led to her own visit to Cadbury. She had taken her dentist along, probably figuring it would be like pulling teeth to get anything out of Amos. But, as Tuttle had told Phyllis Collins, everything had changed now that her husband was dead. It was the way he had died that made Tuttle especially anxious to see Phyllis Collins face-to-face.

"Is that coffee you're drinking?"

"It's from this morning."

"No problem."

She went into the kitchen and came back with a mug. It was pretty bad. But then the coffee Hazel brewed had spoiled Tuttle.

"Have the police been here yet?"

"They came to tell me about Stanley."

"They'll be back. Your husband was killed with his own car. Whoever did it returned the car to the lot. And took the keys."

She said nothing, looking at him.

"The dark lining to your silver cloud is that it seems to give you a motive for getting rid of your husband."

She rose to her feet in anger. "What a dreadful thing to say!"

"Mrs. Collins, I am merely acquainting you with the suspicious police mind. As your lawyer, I have an obligation to prepare you for these things."

She sat. "That is the silliest thing I ever heard."

"Of course it is. That is why you must be ready to tell them— when they ask, don't volunteer it—where you were when your husband was struck by the car."

"I was in bed."

"I know."

"How do you know?"

"The manager of the Frosinone Hotel is a friend of mine."

"Why, you sneaky little man."

Tuttle held up his left hand. He held the mug of coffee in his right. "If the police learn that you and Dr. Jameson spent the night at the Frosinone that will be an airtight alibi."

"I can't have that public knowledge!"

"Perhaps it won't come out. Just say that you were in bed at that time."

"But what if they find out?"

"The manager of the Frosinone is not likely to volunteer that kind of information to the police. Did Jameson pick the hotel?"

"I really don't want to talk about this."

"Whatever you say to me is protected by the lawyer-client privilege."

"That doesn't make it any easier."

"Imagine if I hadn't mentioned this, and the police learned of it and put it to you as a question, and you were wholly unprepared."

She moaned at the thought.

"You haven't any idea where your husbands keys are, do you?"

"No!"

"Sometimes wives and husbands have a spare set of keys to their spouse's car."

Her eyes widened. Her purse was on the table beside her. She grabbed it, opened it, and began to search. Her groping hand stopped, and she looked at him.

"Found them?"

She brought them forth. "I didn't know they were there."

"Better let me keep those for you."

She flung them at him as if they burned her hand. He quickly doffed his hat and caught them in that. He transferred them to a jacket pocket and rose. From his hat he fished a calling card.

"If the police talk to you, if they come here, and if things get rough, just shut up and call this number."

"You're frightening me."

"Lady, I am trying to protect you." He had his tweed hat on his head again. He smiled. "Think of the bright side. You are about to come into a fortune."

22

"How you holding up?" Bob Oliver asked his sister.

"I still can't believe it."

"May he rest in peace."

Phyllis looked at him sharply.

"I mean it. If nothing else he left you rich."

"Is that why you're here?"

How to put it? Her infidelity seemed less serious now, reduced from adultery to fornication after the fact. Ever since his conversation with Primo Verdi, Bob had wondered if Phyllis's fooling around with Jameson could become an obstacle to her getting Stanley's money. It was just because that didn't make sense that it bothered him. The intricacies of the law were at war with common sense. The closest thing to an heir beside Phyllis was himself. But if Verdi told Tuttle, and Tuttle talked, and George Sawyer heard of it, God only knew what complications might arise. George Sawyer, it emerged, stood to make a packet on an insurance policy that the firm had on Stanley. In death, Stanley was becoming a real Santa Claus.

"You and Jameson going to get married?"

She smiled coyly. "I am eligible."

"More than eligible, with all that money."

"David has plenty of money of his own."

"So why did he take you to the Frosinone?"

A lie was forming on her lips when she thought better of it. She looked disgusted. "Was it Tuttle who told you?"

"Tuttle!"

"He's a friend of the manager."

"Phyllis, that could be your alibi."

"My alibi! That's what Tuttle said."

"Why in hell are you talking with Tuttle?"

"He's my lawyer."

"Tuttle is the laughingstock of the bar."

"David trusts him."

"David is an idiot."

"I'll tell him you said so."

He thought a minute. "Maybe it's better so many know of your night at the Frosinone. The police will hear of it and that lets you off the hook."

"That's nonsense. No one would suspect me of such a thing."

"You don't know the police mind."

"I know my own."

"When do you get the money?"

"Is that all you can think of?"

"How much is it?"

She looked at him narrowly. "What's it to you?"

"Well, as you said, Jameson has a pile. I don't."

Her laugh was not encouraging. Even more disturbing was the fact that she was consulting Tuttle. Bob decided to have a talk with the little lawyer.

He wasn't in the press room at the courthouse. The woman who answered the phone at his office sounded like a lady wrestler.

"I am the brother of Mrs. Collins."

"She is a client of ours."

"So she tells me. Could I speak to Tuttle?"

"I could have him phone you."

"He's not there?"

He was in the dining room of the Frosinone, with Peanuts Pianone, so Bob postponed talking to the lawyer. When he did, he asked him if brothers were their sisters' heirs.

"That depends."

"On what?"

"Something happening to the sister."

Bob wished he had asked someone else.

"Of course I know the Rendezvous," George Sawyer said in reply to Cy Horvath's question. "It's a favorite spot of mine."

"I'm not surprised. I took my wife there one night."

"Not many men are there with their wives."

"Oh?"

"The better to sin in their hearts with Wanda Janski when she sings."

"Is it the songs, the singer, the place, the booze?"

"Why choose? It's all of them, I guess."

"I understand Stanley Collins liked the place."

"He was an habitue. When he wasn't a son of an habitue. But speak well of the dead."

"Wanda certainly does."

"You talked with her?"

"I'm talking with everyone who could cast light on Stanley's death."

"And so you're talking to me."

"Who could have known him better than a partner?"

"Or less. A business partner is like a wife in many ways. I suppose any partnership becomes a marriage of convenience. Two people tied together, and you don't know which is keeping the other afloat and which is trying to drown them both."

"Will you sink or swim without him?"

"I'll miss the rascal."

"Who do you think did it?"

"I've been thinking of little else. Could it have been his lady-wife? That was my first thought. *Cui bono?*"

"Is that Cher's husband?"

Sawyer thought about it. "Don't go on the stage, Horvath. As a comedian, you'd make a good cop."

"You mean she would profit from his death."

Sawyer nodded and what was left of his thin hair rose and fell on his freckled scalp. "She is going to be one merry widow with what Stanley left her."

"He was that successful?"

"As a businessman? Ha. I'll answer my own question. I kept him afloat. If I had an ounce of brains I would have cut loose from him long ago."

"Why didn't you?"

"Inertia. It would be bad publicity, largely because you can't tell the truth about such a breakup. Another way a business partnership is like a marriage. Divorces can be messy."

"How long had you known him?"

"A lot longer than his wife had. We were in school together."

"Where?"

"Marquette. Before that at a military school that no longer exists. We called it West Pointless. That was in Wisconsin, too. A boarding school."

"Why real estate?"

"Someone said property is theft. The fact is it changes hands almost as much as money, and someone has to handle the transaction."

"And take a cut?"

"Sometimes it's less than a laceration." Sawyer winced. "I better not go on the stage, either. The agent is a middleman, trying not to get excluded. Did you ever take logic? Either a proposition is true or its opposite is, one or the other, no in-between. The law of excluded middle. You operate on the principle as a cop, whether you know it or not. You're talking to the people who knew Stanley, more specifically, those who were at the Rendezvous that night. Why? Of any of them it can be said, either he—or she—killed Stanley or he—or she—didn't."

"That's not much help."

"It doesn't tell you which is true, of course."

"That's my job."

"Logic only takes you so far."

"You were there at the Rendezvous that night?"

"I was."

"Anything you can tell me that would help?"

"I wouldn't want to point the finger at anyone."

"Either they did it, or they didn't."

Sawyer smiled. "You're a logician. Who would gain by it? His wife. I would, too, in a way. A burden I'd no longer have to carry. And there was an insurance policy on him. Who would lose? Again, I suppose his wife. He talked about divorcing her, but would he have? If he would have, she loses; if he wouldn't, Wanda."

"Wanda."

"He was nuts about her. So was I, for that matter."

"You both have wives."

"Don't rub it in." But he smiled when he said it. "When you step into the Rendezvous, you step out of the real world. Time is unreal, the present is the past, it's neither day nor night. I think Stanley tried to convince himself that it was the real world, and that he loved Wanda and would spend the rest of his life being sung to."

"How does the widow gain?"

"The famous inheritance. Come on, Lieutenant, surely you've learned of Stanley's great ace in the hole. If he was a drag on the company, if he involved me in his debts, there was always the golden promise. Some day he would be swimming in money and everything would be fine."

"That's why the partnership never broke up."

"I guess. You had to see the expression when he talked of turning fifty and coming into that money. Nothing seemed really serious by comparison. A few crushing debts, a bottom line you could touch with your feet, no matter. When Stanley hits the half-century mark, we're all in clover."

"And now the widow will get it."

"The widow will get it now."

"Everyone's a lawyer."

"Or a comedian. Or both."

Cy had liked George Sawyer better as a logician. Either what he said was helpful or it wasn't. You could sink your teeth into a truth like that.

24

When Agnes Lamb knocked on a door in the line of duty whoever answered wore a look that said, *There goes the neighborhood.* Not because she was a cop, but because she was black. Agnes didn't mind. People who weren't really comfortable with her race went out of their way to be helpful. If it didn't harm them, that is. Phyllis Collins had the look of someone who would be helpful or die trying.

"I hate to bother you at a time like this."

Phyllis sighed. "Everyone says that. The truth is, being bothered is a distraction."

"You realize we are looking into the way your husband died."

"I hope so. It's awful that someone can get run down like that."

"I wonder who did it?"

"So do I! We're supposed to be forgiving, and maybe I could forgive something done to me, but running over Stanley is another thing."

"And with his own car."

"Isn't that strange?"

"More than strange. It can't very well be a hit-and-run if

someone stole his car, ran him down, and returned his car to the parking lot of the Rendezvous."

"Please don't ask me who I think did it."

"And make you do my job? No, my questions are little ones. How many sets of keys were there to your husband's car?"

"How many?"

"Would there have been an extra set somewhere? Here, for example?"

"If there is, I don't know about it."

"Where might they be if there was another set here?"

Mrs. Collins had little choice but to look around. Agnes went with her as she ransacked drawers in the kitchen, looked in the desk in the front hall.

"This is pointless," she said to Agnes. "In the first place, I don't think there is another set of keys."

"I spoke to the dealer from whom he bought the car."

"You are thorough."

"Thank you. He got two sets with the car. That's usually the case. You lose one key, you have a backup."

"Maybe it's at his office."

"We thought of that. She searched pretty thoroughly."

"She?"

"Shirley Escalante, the office manager."

"And found nothing?"

"Nothing."

"Maybe Stanley lost the first set and was using the backup."

"I never thought of that."

Phyllis shrugged.

"How about his clothes?"

Phyllis looked abject. "People tell me I should get rid of his clothes, not become morbid and leave everything just the way it was, you know."

"Did you get rid of the clothes?"

Phyllis looked at her. "I have the feeling you already know I haven't."

"I did check Goodwill and St. Vincent de Paul's."

"They're upstairs."

"I'll be along in a minute. Is that a bathroom?"

It was. Phyllis went upstairs and Agnes opened and closed the bathroom door and then went back to the living room. There had been a small black purse on the shelf of the hall closet. She opened it wide and held it to the light, juggling the contents. Bingo. She closed the purse, went to the bathroom and flushed the toilet, then went upstairs.

Phyllis was seated on a bed, surrounded by men's clothes, weeping her heart out.

"Never mind. You should have a friend or relative with you when you do that. Let's go down. I've had a better idea."

"What is it?"

"I'll tell you downstairs."

"Well?" Phyllis said when they were in the living room again.

"When you went upstairs I looked in your purse."

"You had no right to do that."

"Mrs. Collins, the keys we've been looking for are in your purse."

The woman's reaction surprised Agnes. Her laughter did not seem at all forced.

"Is that so? Well, let's take a look."

She dumped the contents of her purse on the couch, shaking it to show it was empty. "These are my keys," she said triumphantly, holding them up.

"And the other set?"

Her eyes dropped to the couch and another set of car keys. Her mouth opened in shock.

"You put them there!"

Agnes just looked at her.

"This is the purse I carried at the funeral. I almost never use it."

"Maybe that's why you forgot about those keys."

Hazel was a creature of moods, and at the moment her mood was triumphant. Several times she had caught Tuttle in a mammalian embrace, and once he had narrowly escaped being kissed by his Amazon secretary. In her eyes, he was no longer the inept and comical excuse for a lawyer, but a shrewd practitioner on to a good thing.

"Let me read your palm, Tuttle. It could tell us things."

"No."

He retreated into the inner office, bracing his shoulder against the closed door lest she follow. But there was only the sound of humming from the outer office. Tuttle glanced at his palm, wondering what it might reveal to the discerning eye. He didn't want to know. He had no curiosity about his destiny, not if it were readable in the creases of his palm. The recent turn of events was due to his own efforts, and he would not allow that some fated sequence had been unraveling.

The phone rang, and Hazel answered it in the outer office. A moment later there was a rap on his door. She looked in and whispered, "Your client."

Tuttle picked up the phone, and almost immediately his ear was filled with the excited voice of Phyllis Collins. She seemed to want him to come immediately.

"Take it easy, take it easy. I'll be right there."

Tuttle could hear Hazel breathing into the phone.

Phyllis said, "I'm being framed."

"I'll be there in minutes."

Hazel's expression was not what it had been when he hurried through the outer office. "What is she talking about?"

"You know as much as I do."

"Is that supposed to be a compliment?"

The old Hazel was back. Frailty, thy name is woman. Tuttle thundered down the stairs and drove to the home of Phyllis Collins.

She was a lot calmer face-to-face, showing him the purse from which the keys of Stanley's car had mysteriously emerged, the purse she had carried at Stanley's funeral.

"You were right to call me. I'll get on it right away."

"You have to tell them I already gave you the keys."

"But there was another set in that purse."

"She must have put them there. Someone did."

To divert Phyllis from the demand that he tell the police he had taken Stanley's keys from her, Tuttle encouraged her to think the worst of Agnes Lamb. Not that he believed she would have planted the keys.

"Who else could have put there there?"

She looked at him with narrowed eyes, their mascara ravaged by her angry tears. "Do you still have the keys I gave you?"

Tuttle nodded. He could feel them in his pocket and they seemed to grow, becoming the massive key to the dungeon in which he would be shut up if Phyllis decided to tell the police about the keys.

"Did she ask where you were the night your husband was killed?"

"I told her nothing. I remembered what you said."

"Good. Anyway, what's wrong with a wife having keys to her husband's car?"

Phyllis obviously hadn't yet seen the significance of her having them.

"What did Officer Lamb say when the keys were found?"

"When I accused her of putting the keys in my purse, she said I could go with her downtown and lodge a formal complaint."

"They're playing games."

"I don't want to play games. I want to be left alone."

"I guarantee it."

And off he went to police headquarters downtown. As if to prove the urgency of his task he went through two red lights, horn blaring, without incident, and pulled into a handicapped spot in front of the courthouse. He was ten feet from his car when he realized he had left it running. He went back, turned it off, and headed for the courthouse steps, his car keys in his hand. Somehow they seemed an omen.

They were. He stood before Agnes Lamb's desk while she told him the story. She had found the keys to Stanley's car in Phyllis's purse.

He told Agnes Lamb he wanted to talk with Phil Keegan.

"What for? It's my case."

"I'm surprised you didn't arrest her."

Agnes made a face. "For having a set of keys to her husband's car?"

She seemed sincere. The point of this visit was to find out what significance was attached to the fact that Phyllis had a set of keys to Stanley's car. Agnes's disinterest reassured him.

"Where do you get your clients?"

"From central casting."

Outside, a police tow truck had pulled up in front of Tuttle's car and was proceeding to rig it for towing. Tuttle ran to stop them.

"Drop the chains! I am an officer of the court and this is an emergency."

Tuttle had handled court cases in less time than it took him to persuade the crew that they were putting themselves in jeopardy if they so much as touched his car. The driver of the truck was half again as high as Tuttle and his partner wasn't much smaller. But Tuttle was filled with righteous anger. He remembered his cell phone and put through a call to Phil Keegan. There was a moment's silence after he explained what was happening on the street outside.

"Tell them your handicap, Tuttle."

"I don't golf."

Keegan guffawed. "Let me talk to one of them."

Tuttle handed his phone to the driver who seemed unsure which end to put to his ear. He listened, gave the phone back to Tuttle, and got into his cab, without even saying good-bye. His partner was more reluctant to call it a day but he got into the cab, too. Tuttle, not without a flourish, opened the door and got into his car. He honked when he passed the truck, cutting sharply in and getting a honk from the truck.

"You have to know how to handle these people," Tuttle said, after telling Phyllis how he had cowed them at headquarters.

"Did she keep the keys?"

"I'll get them later."

Tuttle was beginning to hate those keys. He got the other set from his pocket and handed them to Phyllis.

"There's no longer any point in my keeping these."

She took them as if they were hot and dropped them into her purse, not the little black one but a capacious bag with a wide shoulder strap. Tuttle felt as if he had just destroyed the evidence of his own malpractice. It seemed to be a good time to put the fear of God into Phyllis Collins.

"You may have to tell them where you were that night."

When she understood, she cried, "Never."

"It's no accident that they kept the keys. Of course you can understand how their minds work."

He explained it to her. It was becoming common knowledge that Phyllis had benefitted from her husband's death. And she would have suffered if he had gone on living, divorced her, and cut her off from his prospective fortune.

"You've got a set of keys to his car. You know where he hangs out. You go there, find his car and—"

"Stop."

"The police won't stop once they get going on it. The only way to make those keys insignificant is to produce your alibi."

"I will not tell them David and I were spending the night in a seedy hotel when Stanley was killed."

"Would you rather be accused of running him down?"

"No one would believe I'd do such a thing."

"Mrs. Collins, they could find out about the hotel whether you tell them or not. Someone might have seen you there. You checked in, the clerk will remember and might think it is his civic duty to save you from an unjust accusation."

She fell silent. Then she said in a small voice. "He wouldn't be much help."

"He could prove where you were when your husband was killed."

"No he couldn't. I told you! We left before midnight."

Tuttle sought to conceal that he had, indeed, forgotten. "So you're sticking to your story that you and Jameson checked in there for the night and left before midnight."

"I can't explain."

"You checked out?"

"We just left. The manager saw us go out."

"What did you do, have a fight?"

"I don't want to talk about it."

"You have to tell your lawyer everything."

"I do not. I won't."

Not for the first time, Tuttle was glad he had decided not to handle divorces, urged to this by his father, no matter the loss of income it entailed. Men and women who had been in love hated with an intensity not to be equaled, and even while hating the one they had loved, they got caught up with someone new. And there was all this sneaking about, meeting in hotels, making a sordid trail out of one marriage and into another, probably equally doomed. Phyllis had shut up like a clam, and he had no desire to pry the truth out of her.

The collapse of the case against Phyllis Collins began when her stay at the Frosinone with David Jameson the night her husband was killed was investigated. People seemed to line up to make sure the police knew of this. It was Tuttle who first told Cy Horvath.

"I don't want my client harassed."

Before Cy Horvath checked out the claim, Bob Oliver took him aside.

"I know Phyllis is the gainer, Horvath, but she did not run down Stanley."

"Is that right?"

"What I am going to tell you has got to remain confidential."

And so Cy was told for the second time that David Jameson and Phyllis Collins had checked into the Frosinone the night Stanley Collins was run over. At the hotel, Primo Verdi confirmed it.

"That's right, Lieutenant. Here's the registration card."

"Jones?"

"I also recorded his credit card." Verdi got out a slip and showed it to Cy. "He didn't want to give me that, but it was the only way he was going to get a key to the suite."

Jameson had paid cash and registered as Daniel Jones but the credit card was recorded to cover any other possible expenses.

"What other expenses? He brought his own woman."

Verdi seemed surprised that Cy knew of the escort service run out of the Frosinone. Not that anything would be done about it. The Pianone family protected the hotel from the police, thanks to their arrangement with Chief Robertson.

"I registered him myself."

The whole thing was beginning to sound like a fabricated alibi. Tuttle and Verdi were hardly the kind of witnesses that drove doubt from the mind. And Bob Oliver would want to protect his sister.

"So they spent the night here?"

Verdi smiled slyly. "I didn't say that."

He took obvious pleasure in recounting the early departure of the illicit couple.

"Just a quickie?"

"If he didn't get cold feet. The guy looked like an altar boy, and he was jumpy as a cat when he registered. He didn't even say good-bye when they left."

"Before midnight?"

"It wasn't eleven o'clock."

This gave Cy two choices. He decided to talk with Jameson and leave the widow to Agnes.

The waiting room at Jameson's clinic was full of patients and the dentist was hard at work. The receptionist opened a book when Cy said that he wanted to see Dr. Jameson.

"The soonest I can get you in is two months from now."

"I want to see him now."

"Now?"

He showed her his identification, and she backed away from the counter. She glanced at the waiting patients and said in a whisper, "Come with me."

Cy followed her down a hallway where she opened the door of an office. "Wait here."

Several minutes went by and then a nurse came in.

"Can I help you?"

"Who are you?"

"Dr. Jameson's nurse."

"I came to see him."

"He is with a patient."

"This is important. I told the receptionist who I am."

"But what's it about?"

And then Jameson came in, stripping off latex gloves as he did. He looked at the nurse. "I'm through with Mrs. Molari, Bridget."

The nurse seemed reluctant to go. She showed more apprehension than Jameson did. But she left, reluctantly. Jameson sat behind his desk.

"You're a policeman?"

Cy showed him his identification. Jameson took it and examined it carefully, then handed it back. He looked at Cy, waiting.

"We are examining the death of Stanley Collins. It appears that he was deliberately run over."

"I know Mrs. Collins, but I never met her husband."

"And we know that you checked into the Frosinone with her the night he was killed."

Jameson wiped his face with both hands and then avoided looking at Cy. "My God," he murmured.

"It's true?"

The dentist nodded.

"Of course, when we learned that, there seemed no reason to imagine that his wife could have had anything to do with his death."

"Certainly not!"

"The problem is, you left the Frosinone before eleven o'clock."

"Yes, we did! Because nothing happened. It was a moment of weakness, but we both saw the wrongness of what we were doing before it was too late." Jameson looked at Cy as if expecting praise.

"And left the hotel."

"Yes."

"And then?"

"I took Phyllis—Mrs. Collins—home."

"Immediately?"

"Yes. It was a very emotional time, for both of us."

"Did you stay with her?"

"I took her to her door, and we parted." He sighed. "When I think of all the precautions I took so it would never be known. I even rented a car for the night."

Cy said, "So you cannot really account for her activities after you left her at her door?"

"Lieutenant, you can't be serious. I know she stayed home."

"How do you know that?"

"I telephoned her."

"When was that?"

He thought. "Between one and two. And she had been asleep when I called."

"That would seem to leave her in the clear."

"Of course." Jameson rose to his feet. "I am glad to have been of help, Lieutenant. Now I must get back to my patients."

And so it might have ended. Agnes's report on her conversation with Phyllis Collins corroborated Jameson's story. Yes, they had gone to a hotel but they had left within an hour.

"Did she say why they left?"

"Should I have asked?"

"I would have."

"Cy, the woman was embarrassed to tears as it was. What did you find out?"

"That Dr. Jameson is a very busy dentist."

When Cy told Phil Keegan what he and Agnes had learned, the captain shrugged.

"I never thought she did it, Cy."

"Someone did."

"Have you asked around at that nightclub?"

"I took Marge there one night."

"No kidding. What's it like?"

"We enjoyed it."

Phil might have been trying to remember what it was like to have a wife he could take places. But he had been a widower for a long time.

"Check it out again, Cy."

It was the obvious next step. No, it was like going back to square one and starting again. Cy found himself almost disappointed that the alibi for Phyllis Collins was so tight. He had been as disinclined as Phil to think that she had done it, but the neatness with which she had been excluded was unusual. Most alibis have a hole or two in them, and that has a way of lending them plausibility rather than not. But the night at the Frosinone, even though it had been shorter than one might have expected, put Mrs. Collins in the clear. Whatever one thought of Bob Oliver, Tuttle, or Primo Verdi, the testimony of David Jameson, testimony he had been deeply ashamed to give, clinched it. So back to the Rendezvous it was.

Phil Keegan was in a melancholy mood when he told Father Dowling of the keys that had been found in Phyllis Collins's purse.

"Is it so rare for a wife to have a set of keys to her husband's car?"

"She denied having them."

"I suppose one could forget such a set of keys were about the house."

"They were in her purse."

Phil spelled out what had gone through Agnes Lamb's mind. A couple on the brink of a divorce that would have cut the wife off from any share in the husband's promised inheritance, but the wife would be sole heir if her husband conveniently quitted the earth.

"It is difficult to imagine Phyllis Collins as a cold-blooded murderer."

"You, Roger?"

The priest laughed. He had often assured Phil that anyone was capable of anything, given the right circumstances.

"Oh, I suppose she might have thought about it. But surely Agnes would have asked where Mrs. Collins was on the fatal night."

"She said she was in bed."

"Not improbable, given the hour."

"She implied that it was her own bed."

Father Dowling's eyebrows lifted.

"It turns out that she and David Jameson, her dentist, were checked into a not terribly fashionable hotel."

"Well, well."

Dangerous territory, this. An abject David Jameson had confessed as much in this very room, confessing to the intention and not the deed.

"When we were alone, I realized what I was doing, Father. I had cast myself in the role of her protector and advisor, and there we were together in a sleazy hotel after a series of subterfuges. Nothing happened, nothing that we planned, but I went there with the full intention to commit adultery."

David Jameson seemed to relish the role of penitent. Father Dowling said what a confessor usually says on such occasions.

"Thank God you didn't go through with it."

"I actually thought of you when we were going up in the elevator. I recalled conversations we'd had here in this room. I had become a stranger to myself."

"It is well that you feel such contrition, but you must not underestimate God's mercy."

"I actually fell on my knees and prayed in that hotel room."

The sin, such as it was, had been confessed, and Father Dowling would have preferred the usual surge of relief in the penitent, the eagerness to amend his life and move on. Not brood about what had been confessed. But Jameson was loath to have his sin regarded as somehow of a second order.

"Father, I am a virgin."

The application of this word to a male had always struck Father Dowling as inapt.

"Well, your companion was not."

"The worst of it is, I feel that I deliberately led her astray."

From the account he had given, Jameson's role seemed the passive one. Now he wanted to heap ashes on his own head.

"At any rate, you can make the future unlike the past. Now she is eligible. You mentioned that you had spoken of marriage."

"I can't believe she would have me now."

"Why don't you let her decide that?"

Jameson looked down. "The truth is I wouldn't want her now. I am so ashamed."

"Have you seen her since . . ."

"Of course. I flew to her side as soon as I heard what had happened to her husband. You must have noticed me at the wake and funeral."

"There you are. I am sure she appreciates your loyalty."

"She is going to come into a good deal of money. Will she think me mercenary?"

Socrates started a good deal of trouble when he said that the unexamined life is not worth living. Father Dowling had met too many like David Jameson, who examined their lives to a fault. Introspection is a trap for some. Father Dowling reminded himself that as a confessor, he was not acting in his own name, and he wondered what Our Lord would have done with such a penitent as this.

"I will give you absolution now, David."

Jameson fell to his knees on the study floor and Father Dowling pronounced the formula of absolution.

"And what is my penance, Father?"

His tone suggested he was hoping to be assigned a barefoot trip in sackcloth to some sacred place, the more distant the better.

"Say a rosary for the woman involved."

"Father, I pray for her every day."

When he helped David to his feet, he could not help remembering the graphic description the penitent had given of the failed tryst in the Frosinone Hotel. Finally, he sent him on his way. He must have canceled appointments to come to the rectory. It wasn't Wednesday.

So, when Phil Keegan mentioned that Phyllis Collins had checked into a hotel with David Jameson, Father Dowling could not indicate that this was already known to him.

"How about that guy? I never did trust him. Too pious."

"There but for the grace of God, Phil."

"I know, I know. But isn't that a heck of an alibi for Phyllis Collins?"

"She's off the hook?"

"No matter what you say, I agreed with Agnes that she was a likely prospect. God knows she had motive. And I don't mean his philandering. She was no Easter lily herself. But all that money could prompt her to run him over."

Would the police discover that the errant couple had spent only an hour in that hotel room? What would Phil say if he knew that Phyllis Collins might have had opportunity as well as motive?

"The question is, who else is there?"

"You must have a list."

"It turns out those keys weren't as incriminating as they seemed."

"Oh."

"There was another set, at his office."

"Really."

"That's three sets. One was found on the body."

"Did Agnes find out about the ones in his office?"

"The office manager told Cy. A girl named Shirley."

Tuttle kept in close touch with Phyllis Collins lest Amos Cadbury make a move that excluded the lady's lawyer. It was all too easy to imagine what the patrician Amos Cadbury might say about Tuttle that would prompt Phyllis Collins to cut him loose. He said all this aloud to Peanuts and was almost surprised to find that his old friend was actually listening to him.

"They sent her out to interview her."

"Her?"

"Her!" Peanuts snarled, and it was clear that he meant his black nemesis on the force, Agnes Lamb.

"She went to interview Mrs. Collins days ago."

"This was today."

"Today?"

Peanuts nodded. It wasn't that Peanuts was anxious to work for his salary nor that normally he cared about being the beneficiary of Negative Action so far as the Fox River police department was concerned. But his racist reaction to Agnes's rise in the detective division did not require consistency to be vehement.

"When?"

"She's probably there now."

They had been on their way to lunch but now Tuttle gave Peanuts directions to the Collinses' house.

"I thought we were going to the Great Wall?"

"We will, we will. But I have to see my client first."

At the house, he left Peanuts in the car and hurried up to the door. There was no other vehicle on the street that suggested Agnes was there. Phyllis Collins looked out at Tuttle through the screen door.

"Have the police been here?"

"Come and gone."

"We have to talk."

"Are you the one who told them?"

Aha. So it had been about her night at the Frosinone with Dr. Jameson.

"Let me in."

She hesitated but finally unlocked the screen door. Tuttle hurried inside.

"Do you wear that tweed hat all year round?"

Tuttle took it off. "It's good luck. It was Officer Agnes Lamb who came, wasn't it?"

"You should know, you sent her."

"Whatever I did or didn't do, it was to protect your interests. I told you how the police mind works. It was important for them to learn that you were in the clear."

"If they take my word for it."

"Tell me all about it."

Tuttle listened as to a script he had written. Sooner or later, the police would have learned that she and Jameson had been to the Frosinone the night her husband was killed. This had been a preemptive strike. The fact that the couple had left the hotel before midnight had seemed to blow the alibi out of the water, but Tuttle was sure that Phyllis Collins had convinced Agnes that she and Jameson had a quarrel, he took her home, and that was that.

"Have you any idea how embarrassing it is to talk about it with a stranger?"

She meant Agnes. She wasn't embarrassed enough for Tuttle. Imagine a married woman going off to a hotel with her dentist, even if her husband had been unfaithful. The relations between men and women baffled Tuttle, and the predatory Hazel did not increase his understanding. Of course, most people do dumb things, but there is dumb and there is dumb. The woman had this nice house, security, a husband who kept coming home whatever else he did. What good did it do her to compete with him in the running-around department?

"Well, it's all behind you now, and that's the main thing. Has Cadbury called?"

"No."

"Good. I will call on him. There's no reason for any further delay."

"Delay? It's hardly more than a week."

There was a photograph on the mantle of the late Stanley Collins, a portrait of a successful Realtor.

"And I will be talking to George Sawyer as well."

"What for?"

"Mrs. Collins, your husband was in business with Sawyer. We will want to work out some settlement."

"Stanley was insured."

"Insured?"

"They both were. In case anything happened to either of them."

Interesting. "So George Sawyer benefits from your husband's death?"

"Stanley would have if anything happened to George."

"Of course. Any idea how large a policy we're talking about?"

"A million dollars."

"A million dollars! Are you sure?"

"I heard them talk about it often enough. Susan and I hated it when they did, but they didn't care."

"Susan."

"George's wife."

Tuttle was thinking that a policy that size could be motive enough to dissolve the partnership.

When he left Phyllis Collins, warning her not to discuss her pending inheritance with Amos Cadbury without her own lawyer being present, he asked Peanuts to take him to Cadbury's office.

"Not until we eat."

"Of course not."

His own appetite made this delay acceptable. It was two in the afternoon when they arrived at the Great Wall, and their waitress seemed irked that they would delay her afternoon break. But the wife of the proprietor came to take their order, displaying her beautiful teeth in a smile that had not required the enhancement of Dr. Jameson's skill. Their order was taken, half a liter of red wine was brought, and surliness lifted from Peanuts's simian countenance. During the meal, Tuttle reviewed for the unheeding Peanuts the case he would make for the transfer of money from the trusteeship of Amos Cadbury. And then inspiration struck. He would suggest that he himself be named the trustee of Mrs. Collins's wealth. Peanuts nodded uncomprehendingly. Tuttle got out his cell phone and called Hazel.

"What's that paralegal's name, Hazel?"

"She's engaged."

"Can't she do two jobs at once?"

"I meant she has a fiancé."

"So what?"

"Tuttle, you're an idiot."

It said something of the emerging modus vivendi between his secretary and himself that Tuttle ignored this remark. He told

Hazel that he wanted all the relevant law on the trusteeship of a client's fortune. Hazel's voice softened.

"We're talking about Mrs. Collins?"

"I have just come from talking with her. Her misbehavior with Dr. Jameson has put her in the clear, and there is no obstacle to her inheriting that money immediately. Of course, if she had been indicted Cadbury would have stonewalled."

"I'll call right now."

Hazel hung up unceremoniously and Tuttle returned his cell phone to his pocket. Peanuts watched it disappear with wary apprehension. But Tuttle himself had no understanding of the technology of the cell phone. For that matter, he did not understand the internal combustion engine. Peanuts was sprinkling rice with soy sauce, the stem of his wine glass held firmly in his other pudgy hand. It was a treat to dine with Peanuts and see untrammeled appetite in play.

Maud Pinske watched Tuttle remove his hat, but she wished it were his head. Tuttle had taken the precaution not to call Cadbury's office in advance to warn of his coming.

"Mr. Cadbury is golfing."

Tuttle's eyes went to the closed door of Cadbury's office. Was he in there practicing putting? Long experience with rejection suggested that he was being told a white lie. A man who golfs will tell white lies, and Maud Pinske would have abrogated the decalogue in her service to Amos Cadbury. Not that she was likely to be required to do this. Tuttle grudgingly conceded the flawless rectitude of his adversary.

"Where does he golf?"

"I wouldn't advise disturbing him at play."

"Why, what does he do?"

"I wouldn't know. I am not in the habit of disturbing him ever."

"Perhaps I should make an appointment."

"I will tell Mr. Cadbury you called. Do you have a card?"

Tuttle had cards in the crown of his tweed hat, but he was disinclined to waste one on Maud Pinske, fearing that it would end in the wastebasket beside her desk.

"I'm in the book."

Outside, Peanuts was asleep at the wheel of the unmarked police car. It would have been cruel to interrupt his post-luncheon nap, and more dangerous than disturbing Amos Cadbury on the golf course. Tuttle's own office was six blocks away, out of the high-rent district. He stood contemplating the dozing Peanuts and felt indecision. Peanuts would not feel abandoned if he left him here. He might not even remember why he was parked where he was. He had drunk most of the red wine himself. Tuttle began to hum as he stood there and with the melody came memories of his boyhood and inspiration. Bailey Street and the Rendezvous were a block and a half away. Still humming, Tuttle sauntered off in the direction of the bar.

Cy Horvath was seated at the bar with a beer before him talking with Joe Perzel when Tuttle joined them and ordered a Dr Pepper.

"You know Tuttle, don't you, Joe?"

"Everyone knows Tuttle."

The little lawyer beamed at this supposed praise and sipped

his Dr Pepper with relish when it came. "I understand that Agnes Lamb has been pestering my client."

"Who's your client?"

"The question is, who is your suspect?"

"What were you doing that Thursday night, Tuttle?"

"Innocent citizens don't remember things like that. I can give you a lead."

Perzel was summoned by another customer, and Cy listened while Tuttle told him of the insurance policies George Sawyer and Stanley Collins had held on one another.

"A million dollars, Horvath. I have it direct from the widow's mouth."

Cy did not indicate that he found this information of interest, but, of course, he did. Hadn't Sawyer mentioned insurance? Like Collins, Sawyer had been a frequent presence at the Rendezvous. In any case, he would have known his partner's habits. The ignition key? Cy remembered his conversation with Shirley Escalante, the secretary at Sawyer and Collins who had also told him of the stormy relation between the partners.

"Thanks, Tuttle," Cy said, finishing his beer and getting off the stool.

"Don't tell him I told you."

It was odd to come out of the dim interior of the bar into afternoon sunlight. What Tuttle had told him could not compete with something Perzel had said before the lawyer showed up. Joe had been telling Cy of the transformation in his oldest daughter.

"At her age, she's still single and no wonder. Look." Perzel smiled and waited for Cy's comment.

"Look at what?"

"My teeth, for crying out loud."

There was a gap between Joe's front teeth that might have been his fortune as a comedian if his eyeteeth weren't out of alignment with everything else, giving him a slightly Dracula-like look.

"What's it matter in a man, Cy? But a woman. Well, all that's been changed. The wife read this story in the paper and showed it to me, and I agreed with her. This was the solution for Estelle. I didn't care what it cost. It was either that or have her on our hands forever. Estelle didn't want to do it. For days we argued about it, her mother crying, Estelle crying. I'm offering to pay for it, and she's crying! Anyway, finally she agreed to see Dr. Jameson. Well, by God, it worked. Cy, the girl is someone else. Her smile is a miracle. And she's finally got a boyfriend!"

"Maybe you ought to have it done."

"Cy, it's no joke for a girl."

"I'm sorry, Joe."

"I'll invite you to the wedding. I even look forward to paying for the damned wedding."

"You should invite Jameson, too."

"Are you kidding? Of course I will. Funny thing, Basil, the night man, says he's been in here."

"Jameson?"

"Jameson. And that isn't what he ordered, either. Came in one night and sat about where you are, according to Basil. Sat right next to Willie Boiardo, the piano player."

"How are Willy's teeth?"

Joe shook his head. "If you had a daughter, Cy, you'd understand."

And then Tuttle came in and took a stool and ordered a Dr Pepper.

This exchange with Joe took precedence over what Tuttle had said. And Cy remembered something else. Jameson had mentioned renting a car on that Wednesday when he took Phyllis Collins to the Frosinone.

In his car, Cy called in and got hold of Agnes and asked her to check out rental car agencies for any record of David Jameson renting a car.

"When?"

"Try last Thursday."

"I'll get back to you."

And she did, before he got back to his office. He was just approaching the police garage when Agnes called.

"Bingo. He rented a car from Hertz. What's it mean?"

"Where is Hertz, at the airport?"

"He rented this from their downtown location."

"Where is it?"

"On Bailey Street."

"Bailey."

She gave him an address that was a block or so from the Rendezvous.

"You onto something, Cy?"

"Who knows? Thanks, Agnes."

He had driven past the garage entrance while they talked. He pulled over and called the Rendezvous and asked for Joe Perzel.

"Joe, the piano player, Boiardo. You know where he lives?"

"Sure. The Frosinone Hotel."

"Thanks. Tuttle still there?"

"I made him pay for your beer."

"But I paid you."

"Tuttle didn't know that."

"This is getting to be a habit," Verdi said when Cy came up to the registration desk.

"What room is Willie Boiardo in?"

"Right now, he's in the ballroom. That's him playing."

Cy crossed the lobby and stood in the entrance of what had once been an elegant ballroom. Far off, at a diagonal, was a grand piano at which Willie was playing. Cy listened for five minutes before slowly crossing the great expanse of the room. It seemed a shame to interrupt. Even without Wanda singing the words, Boiardo's playing brought back a lost world.

Willie looked up when Cy came to a stop beside the piano. He played on for a minute, but the dreamy expression did not leave his face when he stopped.

"Nice."

"Thanks."

"Can I buy you a drink?"

"Who are you?"

"Lieutenant Horvath."

"Lieutenant as in police?"

"There's something you might be able to tell me."

"About what?" The little man was suddenly fidgety.

"About someone else."

"Look, if it's about the Frosinone—"

"It's about a dentist."

Boiardo had a nice laugh. He got up and stuck out his hand. "Willie Boiardo."

"I know. I've heard you at the Rendezvous."

"But you were listening to Wanda."

Cy smiled. "Is there a bar in the hotel?"

"I believe there is."

As they came out of the ballroom, Verdi came toward them. "Can I offer you gentlemen a drink?"

"That's better than paying."

They were the only customers in the Frosinone bar. Cy might have objected to Verdi dealing himself in, but his earlier talk with the manager seemed to give Verdi the right. Besides, it seemed to put Willie more at ease. Willie ordered straight bourbon, and Verdi asked for a brandy Alexander.

"You got Dr Pepper?" Cy asked the bartender.

Verdi laughed. "Why don't you ask for a Nehi?"

"Or a grasshopper," Willie said.

"As in knee-high to?"

"We got Dr Pepper," the bartender said and went away. He doubled as waiter, apparently.

"Last Thursday night or early Friday a man named Stanley Collins was run down outside the Rendezvous," Cy said to Willie.

The pianist nodded. "He was a regular."

"I want to ask you about someone else, someone who sat next to you at the bar during a break."

"You're kidding."

"A big fellow, blond . . ."

"Looks like an altar boy?" Verdi said.

Cy nodded. Their drinks came, and Willie, after a healthy pull on his bourbon, said, "Why would I remember him?"

Verdi pushed back his chair. "Hold on. I've got a picture of him. There was a story about him in the paper by Bob Oliver."

"Get it," Cy said.

"Why else am I standing?"

Willie said, "Do you know how many people come into the Rendezvous? Do you know how many I might sit next to when I take a break? I doubt that I am going to be of any help to you."

"Who knows?"

"What difference does it make if he was there that night?"

"I'm not sure."

Verdi came back, waving a newspaper. "Here it is."

He handed it to Willie, pointing to the story. The little man looked at the pictures, read the captions, nodded. "I do remember him."

"It was the night Stanley Collins was killed."

"I don't remember the night."

"You ever see him in there before?"

Willie shook his head, studying the pictures. "Nor since. Just that once. That doesn't mean he wasn't there."

"What do you think, Horvath?" Verdi asked.

"Think? I'm a cop."

Willie handed the newspaper back to Verdi, who rolled it up and began to slap his knee with it.

"You figure he went there after he left here?"

"Maybe you should enter the academy, Verdi. If you could pass the test." To Willie he said, "You're sure?"

"What's he done?"

"Given beautiful smiles to lots of girls."

Willie had a beautiful smile himself.

After the last patient had left, David Jameson retreated to his office where, collapsed behind the desk, he was overwhelmed by the apprehension he had been holding at bay since Lieutenant Horvath's visit that afternoon. He could interpret what was happening to him as divine retribution for the dangerous game he had been playing with Phyllis Collins, or he could lament the injustice of the suspicions that were directed at him. It was the first interpretation that prevailed.

The cold bath of shame he had felt speaking to the detective about that dreadful night at the Frosinone seemed to cleanse him of the sinful desires he had entertained, masking them as some sort of effort to bring Phyllis back to the church. How delusional that now seemed to him. Nor could he prevent himself from realizing that Bridget's estimate of Phyllis was the accurate one. The woman was an immature flirt, no better than the husband she delighted in abusing. He could feel her painted nails trying to undo his belt as he knelt on the floor of the suite in the Frosinone. Dear God, what a jezebel.

Every memory he had of Phyllis was now distasteful to him. Her half-exposed body in his dental chair, her girlish coyness, her ridiculous way of dressing, and that open mouth whenever he tried to kiss her. He felt that he was emerging from a period of insanity and moral blindness. When he had confessed to Father Dowling, he had been in effect congratulating himself, as if like Thomas Aquinas he had driven from his room with a burning brand the woman sent to tempt him to sins of the flesh. "I am a hypocrite," he murmured half aloud. "A pharisee."

Self-accusation had its own odd appeal and he checked himself before he began to exult in his supposed abasement. More hypocrisy. A sob burbled forth. Lord, have mercy on me, a sinner.

A tap on the door, and the silhouette of Bridget appeared in the doorway. It seemed a moment before her eyes adjusted to the darkened room.

"David?"

"I'm all right."

She came in and closed the door behind her. Even in the dim light her snow-white uniform seemed to glow with the promise of innocence. Why, if he had wanted at last to align himself with a woman, had he not seen the attractiveness of the woman who worked at his side all day. She came and stood beside his chair and put her hand on his left shoulder. He brought his right hand up as if he were crossing himself and lay it atop of hers.

"Bridget, I've been a damned fool."

Her hand patted his shoulder, and his own rose and fell with hers, as if he, in turn, were consoling both her and himself.

"It's all over now."

Bridget surprised him. She knew him better than he knew himself. She could not have been unaware of the fool he had been making of himself, yet apart from that first comment on Phyllis that he had scolded her for, she had said nothing. Yet her whole manner had spoken to him, condemning him, more in sorrow than in anger. And now she said it was all over, and he realized she was right. His soul was finally purged of the poison of Phyllis Collins. No. He must not blame her. Or not only her. What would Bridget say if she knew the extent of his folly? Dear God, if she should ever learn of that night in the Frosinone with Phyllis . . .

"I should have listened to you."

She bent over and brought her lips to his hair, then stood. "Come. I am taking you to dinner."

He rose willingly. He was in a mood to be told what to do, to be led. It was as if he had forfeited the right to be his own master, having used his freedom to make an ass of himself.

"No. I will take you."

"But I'm preparing dinner."

Ah. He had been to her apartment only once or twice and then only for minutes, to drop her off or to pick her up when her car was in the garage. Having crossed the office, she switched on the light as she left.

It was a simple meal eaten in her kitchen—spaghetti, a salad, iced tea—giving the occasion a pleasantly domestic air. Across from him Bridget seemed a beautiful stranger, brisk, competent, in charge. He liked it. Phyllis had clung to him even as she manipulated him. But again he discarded the tendency to blame Phyllis for his descent into folly, to the shame of the Frosinone.

"That was wonderful, Bridget."

She tipped her head to one side. "Hardly a gourmet meal."

"Do you know what a bachelor's meals are like?"

"How would I?"

It seemed a mild accusation, and he liked that, too. How swiftly Bridget could carry him out of the malaise into which he had drifted.

"I feel that I have been lost for months."

" 'Midway in this way of life we're bound upon I woke to find myself in a dark wood, where the right road was wholly lost and gone.' "

"That's beautiful."

"It's even more beautiful in Italian."

"What is it?"

"Dante. The beginning of hell." She smiled. "Really, it's the beginning of his escape from hell."

How had he failed to see what a person Bridget was? Dante! And such perceptive remarks about his predicament!

"I'm afraid I would have to go to some popular song for words."

"Like?"

But he couldn't come up with anything on the spur of the moment. So he told her of the Rendevous and the old ballads Wanda Janski sang.

"Most of them were old when I was young but even so . . ."

"When you were young."

"You'd have to hear her to understand."

"All right."

Her smile was her own and that seemed a bonus. Whenever Phyllis smiled he was reminded of the work he had done on her.

"Would you like to go there?"

"It sounds like wonderful therapy." Again she smiled. She might have been prescribing a remedy for him. "We could look in now."

"You mean it?"

"I always mean what I say."

"I believe you do."

She had changed when they arrived at her apartment, putting a glass of cream sherry in his hand and settling him in the living room before disappearing.

"Can I go like this?"

"You look wonderful."

A wistful little smile as she avoided his eyes. What he would have given if he could erase the months during which he had been infatuated with Phyllis Collins, and this night could indeed be his first exploration of the possibility of shedding his bachelor status.

For his mind did run madly on, as if by an emotional acceleration of his relations with Bridget he could negate the past. Why did it help that Bridget knew, at least in part, what a fool he had been? She put her arm through his as they went out to the car.

31

Father Dowling listened as Phil Keegan brought him up to date on the investigation of the death of Stanley Collins. Phil's account of Jameson's registering at the Frosinone with Phyllis Collins struck a note of amused condemnation.

"Do you know what kind of place the Frosinone is?"

A rhetorical question. Phil went on to describe this bastion of Pianone depravity out of which they ran what was euphemistically called an escort service.

"Roger, all you have to do is rename a vice and it becomes a social service. That place was once the U. S. Grant! It's a kind of sacrilege what they've turned it into."

"So that is her alibi."

"Not quite."

Of course, Father Dowling gave no indication that he had heard in this very study David Jameson's account of his failed effort at adultery. Not that Phil knew the details.

"For whatever reason, they skedaddled an hour after signing in."

"Ah."

"The manager guesses they left at eleven o'clock. So there

went the alibi. Jameson says he took her home and then called her at two in the morning and woke her up. So he's her alibi."

"Gallantry is not dead."

"Maybe not. But Stanley Collins is. Cy kept on it and guess what he found out? Jameson turned up at the Rendezvous that night. So he was in the neighborhood at the crucial time."

"Cy suspects David Jameson?"

"It's pretty hard not to. He said he had been on Bailey Street to return a car he had rented in a failed attempt to cover his tracks, but the car wasn't turned in until the following day. In any case, we know he was in the Rendezvous."

The case against David Jameson was circumstantial, but there was a powerful motive. Not only had he been advising Phyllis about her marriage, he went with her to Cadbury's office to find out what a divorce would do to her prospects of getting at the money Stanley would come into when he turned fifty. Cadbury told them a divorce would cut her off completely from that money.

"Cadbury says she didn't take that very well. Her fear was that Stanley would dump her. He had become involved with the singer at the Rendezvous and talked marriage to her, apparently moved by what Jameson had told his wife about the state of their marriage."

Human deeds, looked at from the perspective of the law, can seem almost abstract. Father Dowling could match the main elements of Phil's accounts with his own memories, and how different they then seemed. Amos had told him of the visit to his office by Jameson and Phyllis Collins. Wanda Janski had confessed her affair with Stanley Collins. And Jameson had abased himself in recounting the truncated night at the Frosinone. In these memories, there were notes of pathos, remorse, and contrition one had to assume were genuine. But to Phil the antics of Jameson were simply one more instance of lust and greed turning a hitherto upstanding citizen into a criminal.

Jameson's liaison with Phyllis gave him access to the ignition key to Stanley Collins's car. Stanley's death put Phyllis in line to inherit all the money he had spent his life looking forward to. Phil's assumption was that, when the dust settled, Jameson would marry Phyllis and thus be able to enjoy the prosperity Stanley had long anticipated.

"He's already a very successful man, Phil."

"Have you ever met anyone who thought he had enough money?"

"You may be right. Do you intend to arrest Jameson?"

"Roger, the guy is a basket case. What we will do is tell him what we have learned and then let him stew. He will crack and make the case even stronger."

"Confess?"

"How can a man like that go on living with such a burden on his shoulders?"

That at least showed an appreciation of David Jameson's character. Father Dowling's skepticism at Phil's scenario was based mainly on the fact that David Jameson had made his confession since the fateful night, and it was unlikely in the extreme that he would have suppressed such a serious sin and imagined that he could be absolved of the others he had confessed.

"You never know about people," Marie said when all this became known to her. "I never let on, but I never really trusted that man. Too pious by half." She inhaled through her nose. "A Holy Joe."

"You certainly concealed your feelings, Marie."

She looked at the pastor sharply. "Don't start."

"Oh, I think you've lost your chance."

* * *

Edna had been elated by the fact that her friend Bridget had at last won the heart of David Jameson.

"He was all she could talk about, Father. You can imagine how she must have felt when he became smitten with Phyllis Collins."

Edna did not yet know the danger Jameson was in, and Father Dowling did not have the heart to tell her. Her delight in Bridget's new relationship with Jameson was in itself so delightful that he could not have crushed it by telling her what the police suspected.

Phyllis Collins came to the rectory, dressed sedately, no longer affecting an age she had long left behind.

"Am I a widow in the eyes of the Church, Father?"

"Why ever not?"

"We were never properly married."

"God is merciful."

The effects of David Jameson's excursion into canon law lingered on. Phyllis insisted on seeing her life in terms of laws that in her case were now moot.

"You spoke of marrying again."

She shook her head violently. "All that's over now."

"I shall continue to remember Stanley in my Mass."

Her eyes rounded. "When I think of him being struck down without the chance of . . ." She stopped. She might have been Hamlet considering the state of his uncle's soul, but from a somewhat different perspective.

"I'll say it again. God is merciful."

"I hope so."

But her thoughts had obviously not yet become self-referential. There was no suggestion that she might confess her sins. Perhaps she did not think she had really done anything wrong. Well, remorse would come. Phyllis's shedding of the dress and manner of a much younger woman was a first step, at least, to growing up.

"She makes a better widow than she did a wife," Marie said.

"That is often the case."

Silence, a sharp look, and then Marie went off to her kitchen. Amos Cadbury phoned to say that David Jameson had called on him and that arrangements had been made to have one of the junior partners represent him if events developed as they threatened to.

The Pianone family was more interested in taking money out of the Frosinone than putting any in for necessary repairs, but finally Primo Verdi had convinced Mario Pianone that the state of the elevators in the hotel put the family at risk. When one of the elevators dropped from the seventh floor, just after one of the escorts had exited it, and ended in a pile of debris at the bottom of the shaft, the condition of the hotel could no longer be ignored.

"We could have been sued out of our shoes if she had been in it," Primo said.

Mario Pianone just looked at him, not liking the inclusive pronoun. But finally he nodded. "Go ahead."

And Primo had gone ahead. He declared all elevators out of service until reliable replacements had been installed, and grumbling girls mounted the seven flights to their rooms. Primo's assurance that it was for their own good had little effect.

"We get the shaft around here no matter what," Flora said.

" 'We'?"

"You know what I mean."

"I know what you better not mean."

"Oh, Primo, you're such a prude."

Jealousy of Flora did seem ridiculous but Primo could not ignore the fact that she seemed to be hankering after the fleshpots of the seventh floor. If they were still married he would have divorced her. Flora was half his age, and he could not pretend that the fires of youth had not died down in him. At his age, he should be enjoying the sexless companionship of a woman who was more friend than lover, but what did he have in common with Flora? The one pleasure they could continue to share with the same zest was drinking. It had been booze that brought them together at first, and now, in this second act of their relationship, it proved to be a lasting bond. The haze of alcohol softened the boredom of his suite, and Flora seemed almost content as nightly they drank themselves into a pleasant stupor before the television set.

Mornings were less pleasant, when Verdi had to go about his duties but Flora slept until noon. When she appeared she showed none of the ravages of the previous night. Verdi came to cherish his solitary mornings. What was a little hangover at his age? When Flora joined him in the dining room for her breakfast and his lunch, their routine became welcome. Afternoons, she tooled around town, hitting the malls, shopping, being, he trusted, a good girl.

One day, when Verdi and Flora were at their table in the dining room and Tuttle and Peanuts Pianone were across the room enjoying their Salisbury steak, Bob Oliver came in. He hesitated between joining Tuttle or Verdi but then decided on the latter.

"Okay if I join you?"

"Three's a crowd."

"Oh, Primo, don't be ridiculous. Sit down, Bob."

Oliver sat. What could Primo say? Flora devoted herself entirely to the unwelcome guest, and it was difficult to forget that Oliver had once known her professionally, so to speak. In his presence, she took on all the mannerisms of her supposedly former way of life, and Oliver sat there grinning like a cat.

"You hear they think Jameson the dentist ran down Stanley Collins?"

"No!" Flora cried, hunching forward, eager for the story, displaying her wares. Verdi could have belted her.

Oliver gave her all the details, as he had picked them up in the press room in the courthouse. Flora listened as if she had never heard anything so interesting in her life.

"You'll probably be called as a witness, Verdi."

"They haven't arrested him yet."

"It's only a matter of time."

"You going to write it up?"

Oliver shook his head. "It's not my sort of story. Besides, there's a conflict of interest."

"How so?" Primo asked.

"Phyllis Collins is my sister."

"Is she really going to inherit a fortune?"

"That's right."

Oliver acted as if he, himself, were the heir. "I may do a story about Realtors, Verdi. Sawyer and Collins had a very interesting mutual insurance policy. That will be the hook I hang the story on."

"Sounds interesting," Verdi said, meaning it didn't.

"It's all in how it's handled."

Oliver ordered the Salisbury steak but left most of it on his plate. Verdi stayed on at the table, not wanting to leave Flora alone with Oliver, but when he was called for a consultation with the crew from the elevator company who were at work in the lobby, he could hardly refuse. When he had nodded through the incomprehensible explanation of the foreman, Verdi told him to do what he thought best. Willie Boiardo came slowly down the stairs.

"You're going to have to carry me up, Primo."

"I could switch you to a room on the second floor."

"I like my room."

Sounds of laughter drifted from the dining room and Willie was distracted.

"Bob Oliver," Primo said. "I hope he gets food poisoning."

"He'd come by it honestly, eating here."

"Hey, I thought you liked it here."

"I like it about as much as you do."

Meaning they were too old to care about moving now. The laughing couple emerged from the dining room, Flora smiling radiantly into Oliver's foolish face.

"Hasn't she retired?" Willie asked.

"Go to hell."

Verdi went seething to his office behind the registration desk. It was the fact that he had no claim on Flora—other than some common memories, a few good and bad times, a shared suite, and boozy companionship—that made him resent the way she flaunted her charms at Bob Oliver. But if he resented Flora, he hated Oliver. He was even mad at Willie Boiardo.

Phil Keegan, Cy Horvath, and Agnes Lamb sat in Keegan's office with Zola the assistant district attorney discussing the case against David Jameson. Agnes had been elected to convince Zola that they had enough evidence to get an indictment. Zola had begun to shake his head halfway through her recital.

"I couldn't sell that to a jury in a million years."

"What's missing?"

"I should explain evidence to you?"

"We don't have a video of him running over Stanley Collins, if that's what you mean." Agnes was peeved.

Phil said, "How about motive, opportunity, being in the vicinity of the crime, having access to the keys to the car, and getting rid of the obstacle to his grand passion for Phyllis Collins?"

There seemed no need to mention the apparent estrangement of the couple, Jameson having transferred his affections to Bridget his nurse.

"You've got as good a case against her," Zola said.

"She was home in bed."

"Any witnesses?"

"Jameson called her at two in the morning and woke her up."

"He's her alibi?"

"That's right."

"And she will probably decide to be his and say he called her every ten minutes from midnight on."

"What would it take to convince you?"

"A witness. And even then, if Jameson could be put in the car, he could say he never saw the man before he hit him. The most we would have is leaving the scene, and we don't have that."

Cy said nothing, just sat there, but the way he looked at Zola unsettled the ADA.

"What do you think, Horvath?"

"He's the best we've got."

Despite his own misgivings, Phil was not about to let Zola dismiss Jameson that easily. "We know we have only circumstantial evidence, Emil. There are people rotting in Joliet on the basis of far less."

"He's been talking to Manny Puliti, the hotshot defense lawyer in Cadbury's firm."

"And you're scared?"

"My interest is justice," Zola said piously.

They were still discussing it when the news about Bob Oliver was brought to Phil Keegan. His secretary whispered in his ear for a minute and then stepped back. Phil told the others.

"Bob Oliver was found in the alley behind the Frosinone. Hit-and-run. They think he was lying there for hours."

"Dr. Jameson, call your office," Zola said.

Nobody laughed.

✂ Part Three ✂

"Bridget, she has no one else. Someone has to stay with her."

"Stay with her?"

David Jameson looked at her with an expression Bridget could not decode. "Think what the woman is going through. First her husband, now her brother."

How could she refuse? But Bridget called Edna Hospers and the two women went together to the Collinses' house where they found Phyllis alone and, it became apparent, a little drunk. Her hair was a tangled mess, and she seemed to have lost one of her slippers, so that red painted toenails emerged from the bottom of her pink housecoat. Thank God Edna had come along.

"You remember me, Mrs. Collins? Bridget, Dr. Jameson's nurse."

She perked up. "Did he come with you?"

Edna said, "Let's get this place cleaned up, shall we?"

Phyllis looked around as if her surroundings were unfamiliar. Edna found an uncapped bottle of gin on the sideboard in the kitchen. Phyllis had followed her there.

"I don't usually drink. It doesn't help at all."

"Have you had any sleep?"

Bridget said, "I think she's been sleeping on the couch in the living room."

Edna took the fingerprinted glass that Phyllis was carrying and poured an ounce or two of gin in it. She added orange juice and handed it to Phyllis. The woman who didn't drink drank it as if it were merely orange juice. Edna took her arm.

"Now you are going to bed."

Bridget stayed on the first floor, thinking that this was where David had come on Wednesdays, and now he had sent her here to be with the woman he had visited then. She could not understand the meaning of it. If Phyllis had been any other patient, it would have been different. But now that David had finally taken notice of her, this renewed concern for Phyllis Collins seemed to threaten what had hardly begun. Would this second tragedy draw him back into the web from which he had escaped?

"How do you know she's alone?" she had asked him.

"I know she is."

"Have you been there?"

His eyes would not meet hers. How weak he was. All men are weak, Edna had told her that. Only another woman can see a woman's wiles, men cannot.

"No. I talked to her on the phone. She doesn't make much sense."

Bridget was still standing in the living room when Edna came down.

"Did she go to bed?"

"She's out like a light."

"The poor thing."

"Bridget, this is what I am going to do. At the senior center I have dozens of old women who would be happy to take turns staying with Phyllis. You have your job and . . ."

David? Bridget wondered if that were so. She had an ally in

Edna, that was certain, but their alliance had been formed when Bridget was the nurse David ignored.

Suddenly it struck her how awful it was to be thinking only of herself. She meant it when she called Phyllis a poor thing. As David had said, first her husband, now her brother. They had the place cleaned up when Officer Agnes Lamb came to the door. She told Bridget and Edna all the police knew.

Bob Oliver had been struck by a vehicle and left for dead in the alley behind the Frosinone Hotel.

"What was he doing at a place like that?" Edna asked.

"Apparently, he sometimes had lunch there. And there's a bar."

It was the fact that Bob Oliver had been killed in the same way as Stanley Collins that was so strange.

"Of course, it could be just a coincidence." But Agnes said it without conviction. "It wasn't the same car, anyway. The one that killed Stanley Collins is still in the police garage."

"Have you found the car that struck him?"

"We think it was a pickup belonging to the crew installing new elevators in the hotel."

It had been parked behind the hotel; the keys had been left in the ignition. It had been found a block away, parked at the curb.

"But why?"

"We're talking to anyone who can help us answer that. I was sent to talk with his sister."

"That's going to have to wait."

"I've talked with her before, you know. About her husband."

"And now her brother."

"Why?"

"That's the big question," Agnes said.

* * *

Bridget explained to David the arrangements for taking care of Phyllis Collins that Edna Hospers had made.

"Won't they be strangers to her?"

"David, I am a stranger to her. Who are her friends?"

He looked blank. "I don't know." He looked at her. "Thank you for going to her."

"She'll be all right."

He turned away, but she put her hand on his arm.

"David, you mustn't feel responsible for her. It is all over, isn't it?"

He swung to her. "There wasn't anything to be over."

"Good."

"I was trying to advise her."

"She's in good hands now."

She moved closer to him, and he put his hands on her shoulders. She pressed against him, and his arms encircled her. He would be just fool enough to be drawn back to Phyllis Collins out of sympathy, and she didn't intend for that to happen, not if she could help it. She and Edna had talked.

"Men are just little boys who have grown up, Bridget. More or less."

How true that seemed. But what are women but grown-up girls?

"It's not the same thing," Edna had assured her.

And then Lieutenant Horvath came, and Bridget stayed in the office, taking a seat.

"I have to ask you some questions," Lieutenant Horvath said. He looked at Bridget.

"It's all right." David's voice was husky.

"Okay."

It was clear that the police had suspected David of being involved in the death of Stanley Collins. Horvath didn't put it so baldly, but that was the implication. Why else would he want to know where David had been on Wednesday when Bob Oliver had been run down behind the Frosinone Hotel?

"He was with me," Bridget said. "The clinic is closed on Wednesdays."

Horvath looked at her, and she could not read his expression. "With you?"

"I volunteer at St. Hilary's. I help out there on Wednesdays. David came with me."

"Volunteer in what way?"

"I work with Edna Hospers."

"I had offered my services before," David said. "I think I may become a regular now."

"Dental services?"

He tried to laugh. "It would be mainly dentures with the old people there. No, I want to do pastoral counseling."

"Did you know Bob Oliver?"

"He wrote a story about my work here."

"That's right."

"The photographs you see around here were taken on that occasion. They took far more than they could use, and we bought them all and had them framed. I can tell you the story was a tremendous boost to my practice. I owed Bob Oliver a lot."

2

Shirley Escalante found the offices of Sawyer and Collins a gloomy place after the death of Stanley. George Sawyer was a busy Realtor, you had to give him that, and he was more often out than in. That left Shirley underemployed, half hoping the phone would ring, counting the hours until five in the afternoon when she could escape. So Bob Oliver's surprising visit had come as a welcome relief.

For one thing he was a man, and he responded to Shirley's enhanced smile. He began by telling her the kind of stories he wrote.

"Maybe you saw the one about David Jameson the dentist."

"You wrote that?" She had seen the pictures on the wall at Jameson's clinic and had read the reprint available in the waiting room.

"That's right. I think I doubled his business for him."

Well, she wasn't going to tell Bob Oliver that she herself was one of the beneficiaries of Jameson's skills.

"So what can we do for you?"

" 'We'? Is Sawyer here?"

"That's the editorial we."

"Hey, that's my line."

She liked him.

"I guess you know Stanley Collins was my brother-in-law."

"He was a wonderful man."

He dipped his chin and looked at her through his bushy brows. "He had quite a reputation."

"He was always a gentleman!"

Bob Oliver held up his palm. "Believe me, I wasn't suggesting anything."

"Don't. Because there wasn't anything."

"Stanley must have been a man of steel."

"He was one of the nicest men I've ever known." However exaggerated, the remark seemed demanded by her loyalty.

"May he rest in peace."

"I went to his funeral."

"Sad, sad. This has been terrible for my sister. It's with her in mind that I have been thinking of doing a feature on Realtors. A kind of tribute to Stanley."

"Oh, that would be wonderful."

"Phyllis suggested it long ago but nothing came of it."

"I'll bet you could make even real estate interesting."

"But agents? Does Mrs. Sawyer still work here?"

"Not since I've been here."

"Post hoc ergo propter hoc?"

"What does that mean?"

"Ask Dr. Jameson. I heard it from him."

"You really are thinking of a story?"

"I would need your help, of course."

Shirley was more than willing to help him. It seemed a posthumous blow struck for Stanley Collins. When Bob asked her to lunch, she said yes. It seemed almost a duty. And he was a pleasant fellow, a little old, perhaps, but then she wasn't getting any younger.

The next day was Tuesday, and he was back with a photographer who shot several rolls of film while Bob Oliver interviewed Shirley. Sylvia Woods wore jeans, a baggy T-shirt, and a Cubs baseball cap. Bob Oliver wanted shots of the offices of the partners.

"Is Stanley's office locked?"

"You can see it."

"Has Phyllis been here since Stanley's death?"

"No, she hasn't."

"You mean no one has been in there since he died?"

"I have, of course."

"Of course. Did Mrs. Sawyer even come by?"

"I can count the times I've seen her here."

"No kidding." But he disappeared into Stanley's office with Sylvia, and Shirley followed. "Sylvia, I want one of the desk. The empty desk. You know."

A nod of the baseball cap. No wonder there had been so many more photographs on the walls of Jameson's clinic than had appeared in the newspaper article. Sylvia seemed to use the automatic-rifle principle in taking pictures.

"Anything else?" she asked.

"You get everything?"

"How about another of you two together?"

She said it in a taunting way, but Bob liked the idea, putting his arm around Shirley's shoulders and tugging her close. "How's this?"

"Actionable."

She packed up her equipment then and loaded bags onto her shoulders. *"Arrivederci."*

"Auf Wiedersehen."

"She's the best," Bob said when Sylvia was gone. "Okay, let me ask you some questions."

He wanted to know about the insurance policy that George and Stanley had on one another.

"My sister told me about it," he said, when Shirley hesitated. "What didn't she tell you?"

"Just tell me what you know of it. Phyllis doesn't have much business sense. She's come into a lot of money from Stanley, but he must have some equity in the firm."

Shirley told him what she knew, not altogether willingly. His interest in his sister's affairs seemed somehow greedy. But someone had to act for Phyllis, and who better than her brother? Shirley began to think that the idea of writing a story about the agency was just a pretext.

In a way, it was even more of a surprise when Susan Sawyer came by the agency a day or so after Bob Oliver's visit. A key turned in the outer door, and there she was.

"Oh, you're here," she said when Shirley rose from her desk.

Mrs. Sawyer was a well-groomed woman carrying a few extra pounds who acted as if she were Shirley's older sister. Her hair was short, graying attractively, and she wore a capacious jacket that fell almost to her knees, neutralizing the weight she carried. Her shoes were sensible flats, laced, crepe-soled.

"It has been ages since I've been here, isn't that awful?"

"There isn't much going on here at the moment."

"You are not suggesting that business has fallen off since Stanley died?" She looked at Shirley as if they shared a secret.

Shirley managed not to answer that. Of course, Mrs. Sawyer would have taken her husband's side in the continuing quarrel between the partners. Shirley's loyalty to the late Stanley Collins had been strained by what came out after he was killed, not that she was surprised at all the talk about what a womanizer he had been.

"Has Phyllis been here?"

"In the office?"

"I meant since . . ."

"No." Shirley remembered the stormy visit when Phyllis had shouted and screamed at Stanley behind the closed door of his office. Perhaps George Sawyer had brought that story home to his wife. "The most exciting thing recently was a journalist's visit."

Mrs. Sawyer had been walking away from Shirley's desk, but now she swung toward her.

"A journalist!"

"He brought his photographer, too. He may do a feature on the agency for the *Tribune*."

She sat across from Shirley and asked to hear all about it. After a while, Shirley felt that she was being grilled. Mrs. Sawyer wanted every detail of Bob Oliver's two visits.

"You just gave him the run of the place?"

"I'm sure it was all right. Of course, they wanted photographs of everything."

Mrs. Sawyer seemed to want to say more, but after a moment she stood.

"Was that Stanley's office?"

Susan tried the door, opened it, and looked inside. Shirley had risen to go with her but the door of the office closed. Shirley half resented the wife of Stanley's partner checking out his office, but what could she say? Twenty minutes went by, and the door remained closed. What was she doing in there? A few minutes later the door opened, but more time passed before Susan Sawyer emerged.

"Did you know I worked with George before he and Stanley became partners?"

"So I understand."

"A long time ago, at least you would think it was. I'm afraid I wasn't much more of a Realtor than Stanley."

"You were an agent?"

"Did you think I was a secretary?" Susan found this amusing. Shirley had half a mind to tell her that her title was office manager.

Susan ran her thumb under the shoulder strap of her large purse and looked around the reception area. "Well, so much for sentimentality."

"Did you and Mr. Sawyer work out of this office?"

"That's right. With Stanley."

Well, the visit gave Shirley something to think about—and resent. It was a sad thought that Stanley had lost the long quarrel between himself and George Sawyer, but Susan's visit, which in retrospect seemed a kind of triumphal tour, made Shirley wonder what difference it all made. Shirley had had no misgivings about letting Bob Oliver look around, but Mrs. Sawyer's visit had taken on the aspects of an inspection tour.

"You do have my old office, you know."

"Really?"

"I think that very desk was mine." She came around the desk and Shirley got up, guessing that Mrs. Sawyer wanted to sit at the desk. She left her there, to have nostalgic thoughts if she wanted, and went down the hall. Ten minutes later, when she came back, Mrs. Sawyer was sitting at her husband's desk, on the phone.

The following day was Thursday, and on her lunch hour, Shirley turned on the radio and heard the dreadful news. She twirled the dial to find out more of what had happened, but the bulletin she had heard was seemingly all there was. On the computer, she brought up the Web site of the *Fox River Tribune*, but there was nothing about the death of Bob Oliver. It wasn't until an hour later that the story appeared. Shirley sat stunned, looking at the chair in which Bob Oliver had sat, looking at the closed door of Stanley's office. Run over! Run over in the same way Stanley had been.

She tried to reach George Sawyer on his cell phone, but he didn't answer, so she called his house. Susan answered.

"Have you heard?" Shirley said.

"Heard what?"

"Bob Oliver has been run over."

A long pause. "Who is Bob Oliver?"

"He's the journalist I told you about."

Phil Keegan had schooled himself against reacting to newspaper accounts of matters under investigation by his department, but the death of Bob Oliver, one of their own, had unleashed the fourth estate, which, likened Fox River to some third world backwater in which citizens were at risk as much from their alleged guardians as from the criminals among themselves.

By a logic whose cogency could only be appreciated by those long immersed in the media, Tetzel in the *Tribune* saw an obvious and necessary connection between the deaths of Stanley Collins and Bob Oliver. He pointed out that the two were brothers-in-law, and he emphasized that the death of Collins, still unexplained by the police, had been drifting into that black hole of forgetfulness that was the destiny of unsolved crimes in Fox

River. And then he forsook facts for fiction and penned a portrait of the killer. He felt no need to establish that the same person had killed both men because killing Bob Oliver was a desperate cry for help. In Tetzel's jeremiad the delinquency of the police lay chiefly in their deafness to this tortured soul's call for his own capture, lest he kill again. Stanley Collins and Bob Oliver became bit players in this psychodrama featuring Tetzel's imaginary troubled killer.

"Maybe we should bring Tetzel in for questioning, Cy" Phil said. "He seems to have all the answers."

Cy ignored this, as he was wont to do. Dealing with the press was in one respect a game and in another a minefield one entered only reluctantly.

"I talked with a fellow named Janski, an accountant at the *Tribune*," Cy said.

"An accountant?"

"Oliver had to justify his expenses to Janski to get reimbursed."

"So."

"So why was Oliver in the alley behind the Frosinone? Janski couldn't say. He thought Oliver was working on Realtors although he had planned a piece on city architecture, and the Frosinone, despite its current reputation, is supposedly a miracle of design. He also mentioned the photographer who worked with Oliver, and I talked with her."

"He couldn't let it go," Sylvia Woods had told Cy. Janski had called her and turned over his office to Cy for the conversation. "He had this thing about local architecture. He could walk down a street and talk your arm off about facades and styles and the great midwestern schools of architecture. He made me feel the way I did in Art Appreciation, wondering if I had ever seen a picture before. Bob Oliver was appalled at the condition of the Frosinone. The fact that they were replacing the elevators seemed to promise more." Syliva popped the top of her bottle of water and took a drink. "You know who owns that hotel?"

Cy said he knew. She leaned toward him.

"My first thought was the Pianones."

"You think they had something against Oliver?"

"I don't know. Look, the fact is I didn't get along with Bob. He was, well, you know, always coming on to me."

Cy could understand that. Despite the haberdashery, Sylvia was a very attractive young woman. "You work with him often?"

"I've done the pictures for all his features. Beginning with the one on the dentist."

"Jameson?"

"Jameson."

"Did you go with Oliver to the Frosinone?"

"Just the once. Then he seemed to junk the whole idea. He gave me a lecture on the hotel's architecture, and I asked him why it wasn't a national landmark if it was so great. That's when he told me the Pianones owned it."

"You think he complained to them?"

Syliva shrugged and played with the cap of her water bottle. "Where would he find them? I've heard about them for years, but they are like a myth, the local boogeymen."

"Don't you know Peanuts?"

Sylvia laughed. "Are they all that cuddly?"

The thought of Peanuts Pianone as cuddly was more than Cy could handle. He let Sylvia go and thanked Gerry Janski when he came to take repossession of his office.

"Janski," Cy said musingly, looking at the accountant. "Are you related to the singer?"

"She's my sister."

"What a voice."

"What a waste, you mean, singing to drunks in nightclubs."

"You ever been to the Rendezvous?"

Gerry shook his head, as if Cy had mentioned a house of ill fame. "Our mother was the organist at St. Hilary's."

"Ah."

At the Frosinone, Primo Verdi was surly and nervous.

"I wish they would stop mentioning the hotel in these stories about Oliver, Horvath. It has nothing to do with the Frosinone."

"Free publicity."

Verdi just looked at him.

"Have you any idea what he was doing in the alley?"

"Maybe he was going to meet one of the girls."

"He ever do that?"

Verdi wrestled with the answer, but nodded.

"Do you know which ones?"

For answer, Verdi picked up the phone, turning away from Cy as he talked into it. He hung up. "She'll be down."

They waited in silence. Of course, Cy knew of the escort service the Pianones ran out of the hotel, but so far as he knew he had never seen one of the girls. The one that came across the lobby from the stairway was red-eyed, and her chin trembled as she approached.

"What the hell's wrong with you?" Verdi asked.

"You know."

Cy took her arm and led her across the lobby. She tried to tug free. "I'm not working."

"Flora, he's a cop, for God's sake," Verdi yelled after her.

She stopped struggling and looked with teary eyes at Cy. "Is it about Bob Oliver?"

"That's right. You knew him?"

She nodded, looking at Cy as if she wondered whether he understood. Cy understood.

"The manager suggested that he might have been in the alley to meet someone."

"Meet someone?"

"I think he meant you."

"What a bastard."

"Oliver?"

"Primo. He was my husband. A real idiot."

"For marrying you?"

"Oh, ha, ha. But, yes, that's true. What kind of man would marry a girl who makes her living on her back?"

"You divorced him?"

"He divorced me. That brought us more or less back together again. But he just couldn't forget about Bob Oliver. You'd think there'd never been anyone else."

"What do you mean he couldn't forget it?"

"Oh, Bob wouldn't let him. At first Primo teased him, but it ended up with Bob teasing Primo. Primo didn't like that a bit. Of course, I was the one who paid for it."

"He beat you up?"

"I'd like to see him try. No, he'd never do that."

"How angry was he with Bob Oliver?"

"I'm not making it up. Ask the bartender. Ask that little lawyer, Tuttle. They've seen it."

"You're crying because of Oliver."

She began to cry again. "Life is so damned sad, isn't it? You want to pretend you can just live now, enjoy it, and tomorrow will be the same. But look where we're all headed."

"Where you from?"

"Bardstown."

"Where's that?"

"Kentucky."

"How you'd end up here?"

"I met Primo in Vegas."

"And he put you to work here?"

"Oh, no. I was already in the life. We really did get married, though. But he was always suspicious, so I gave him reason to be, and he divorced me."

"And you went back to work?"

She looked at him. "Rarely. We're back together again, Primo and me."

"Married?"

"That was a big mistake. We both realize it now. But he couldn't forget about Bob Oliver." She dabbed at her eyes.

"You think Primo ran over him?"

"Why don't you ask him?"

Cy went back to the desk and asked him.

"She tell you that?"

"How would she know?"

"What she doesn't know . . ."

"You and Oliver didn't get along?"

Verdi glared at Flora who was drifting across the lobby toward the bar. "He was always pestering Flora."

"She's young enough to be your daughter."

"She was old enough to marry me."

"To each his own."

Verdi brightened up. "Eddie Howard sang that. Willie Boiardo loves that song."

"It sounds to me like you had reason to run down Bob Oliver."

"When do they think he was hit?"

"It's only an approximation. Midafternoon."

"It doesn't matter."

"Why?"

"I can't drive. Never learned how. Never had to."

Father Dowling heard from Edna of the arrangement she had made for women from the senior center to take turns being with Phyllis. Leave it to Edna to come up with a practical solution.

"They love it. And it lets Bridget off the hook."

"How so?"

"Dr. Jameson sent her to be with Phyllis Collins. She's his nurse. Bridget asked me to go along, and that's when I thought of making a project of it. Bridget helps me out on Wednesdays, you know."

"You bring out the best in people, Edna."

She dismissed this. "But now I had to take him on, too. Jameson."

"He's not much help?"

"Too much help. He likes to pry into people's lives."

"I think I told you once he thought of becoming a priest."

Edna lifted her eyes. "Well Bridget likes him and that's enough for me."

They had been talking in the parking lot behind the former school that was now the parish's center for seniors under Edna's management. They went inside then and from the hallway Father

Dowling saw David Jameson hunched over a table, deep in conversation with old Charley Schwartz.

Edna said in a low voice, "Bridget says the police questioned him about Bob Oliver's death."

"There were those who thought he had something to do with Stanley Collins's death."

"Because of Mrs. Collins."

No need to say anything about that. Bridget rose from a bridge table and joined them.

"I'm dummy. In every sense of the term. They play a cutthroat game."

"I told Father about the volunteers who are spending time with Phyllis Collins."

"I'd rather play cards," Bridget said.

Edna smiled. "You just like being here because David is here."

"He says this is the most fulfilling work he does."

Jameson, noticing the three of them in conversation, rose, said something to Charley, then came toward them. Edna led Father Dowling away.

"He still is not a bird in hand," she explained. "We'll leave them alone."

"Ah."

"Maybe after they're married he will be content to be just a dentist."

"A bit of a pest?"

Edna rolled her eyes. Well, David Jameson had been involved in less rewarding extraprofessional activities in recent weeks, so bothering old people in Edna's center was something of an improvement.

As Father Dowling was leaving, Charley Schwartz called to him. Father Dowling stopped, and Charley shuffled toward him.

"Leaving, Father?"

"That's right."

"I'll come with you."

"To the rectory?"

"I'm going outside for a smoke."

Outside, with the doors shut behind them, Charley lit a cigarillo. Father Dowling took out his pipe and lit it.

"We're a dying breed, Father."

"Oh, you have years ahead of you, Charley."

"I meant us smokers." Charley puffed contentedly for a moment. "Dr. Jameson? He says I'm not too old to have my teeth straightened."

"What did you tell him?"

"I prefer them curled." Charley's smile revealed his amber uppers, the color of a meerschaum pipe.

"It is generous of him to help Edna."

"If you say so. He said to feel free to bring my problems to him. So I did."

"What were you talking about?"

"My cat. I asked him to take a look at her."

"Anything wrong?"

"What's the difference? There's nothing wrong with me and he won't let me alone."

"What did he say?"

"He said he wasn't a vet. I told him I was. Korean War. I was giving him the story of the battle for Pusan when he left me."

Poor David Jameson, Father Dowling thought as he went on to the rectory. How often good intentions are a pain in the neck. He would have to begin a novena that Jameson would marry Bridget and begin and end his charity at home.

With less work to do than usual Shirley Escalante brooded over
the deaths of Stanley Collins and Bob Oliver. The one had been
her employer, and the other had been right here in the office
talking to her the day before he was killed, so she could hardly
expect not to think about them. Gradually a dreadful possibility
occurred to her. Maybe Phyllis Collins benefitted from the death
of her husband, but no one imagined that she had anything to do
with it. Someone else benefitted, too. George Sawyer. And after
Bob Oliver had left her that day after Mrs. Sawyer's visit, George
Sawyer came in, and she told him that the reporter had been
there.

"What the hell for?"

"He does these feature articles in the *Tribune*. He is planning
one on Realtors. The photographer took at least a hundred pictures."

"Of what?"

"The office. Mine, yours, Mr. Collins."

"You let him into Stanley's office?"

"They just took some photographs."

She had half a mind to tell him that his own wife had been in there, too. Mr. Sawyer stormed into Stanley's office, slamming the door shut behind him.

Shirley was stunned. She had expected him to be delighted at the prospect of free publicity. He was banging around in his late partner's office, opening and shutting drawers, grumbling audibly. When he came out he stood in front of Shirley's desk.

"I suppose he asked you a lot of questions."

"He was trying to understand how an agency like this works. They wanted your photograph, too."

"Was he alone in the offices?"

"No! The photographer was with him. I was with him."

He got control of himself. "I don't like people snooping around here. You should have known better."

Shirley was furious. "I thought I was doing something beneficial for the firm."

"Okay. Okay. He wasn't alone in there?"

"No!" What on earth difference would it have made if he had been?

He was about to respond in anger, but he swung away, went into his own office, slamming the door. Shirley escaped to the restroom. When she returned George Sawyer was seated at her desk. He rose.

"I'm going out. You can reach me on my cell phone."

He did not look at her, as if he were ashamed of the scene he had put on. But after he was gone she thought his manner seemed to have been more of guilt than shame. From that moment she was certain he had killed both his partner and Bob Oliver.

The following day this conviction had strengthened. But what was she to do with such knowledge? She had already spoken with Lieutenant Horvath, but she wanted a more sympathetic ear for her story. And she wanted to talk to someone who could persuade her she was wrong if she was. She thought of Father Dowling.

He was the priest who had presided at the funeral of Stanley Collins. At the time, Shirley had entertained thoughts of again practicing her faith, but she had slept late last Sunday as she usually did. Even so, something in the priest's voice and manner made her sure she could talk to him and tell him the awful suspicions she had about George Sawyer.

The woman who answered the rectory door was a bit of a surprise. Did Father Dowling's mother act as his housekeeper?

"At the moment, he's over at the school," the housekeeper said when Shirley asked if she could speak with Father Dowling. "Of course, it's no longer a school. We use it now as a center for older people. You can wait here in the parlor." She came in with Shirley, got her seated, and then sat herself, smiling receptively.

"Are you his mother?"

"Mother? Whose mother?"

"Father Dowling's."

"My name is Marie Murkin. I am the housekeeper." She had gotten to her feet. Her smile was gone.

"Oh, I'm so sorry."

"Have you ever met Father?"

"I've only seen him from a distance."

The frown went even if the smile did not return. "When you see him you will see why your question surprised me." Again she sat. "Do you live in the parish?"

"I think so."

"Don't you know?"

"I don't belong."

"But you want to. Is that why you're here?"

Shirley had not been prepared for this. She tried to imagine herself quizzing clients at Sawyer and Collins like this. The thought led her to tell Marie Murkin where she worked.

"Really! You worked for Stanley Collins?"

"And for his partner, George Sawyer. I am the office manager."

There was the sound of a door opening, and a moment later the priest stood in the doorway. Marie Murkin had risen.

"Father, this is the office manager at Sawyer and Collins."

He came toward her and took her hand.

"My name is Shirley Escalante. I have to talk with you."

"Is that all right, Marie?"

The housekeeper gave out an unconvincing little laugh and hurried down the hallway. Father Dowling closed the door and took a seat at the desk. "Well then?"

"I don't know where to begin."

"Why not try the beginning."

"Well, I do work at Sawyer and Collins. And, of course, you know what happened to Mr. Collins."

He nodded. She had been right to think that she could tell him everything, and she did. Because somehow it did seem the beginning, she started with the key to Stanley Collins's car.

"I had an extra set in the office, but when the police asked about that I couldn't find them. They were gone. Other than George Sawyer, no one else would have known of those keys."

"And you think he took them."

"Their partnership was an endless quarrel. Somehow they remained friends of a sort but in the office it was constant wrangling. Most of it initiated by George Sawyer, who thought Mr. Collins did not carry his weight in the agency."

"Was that true?"

She wished she could deny it, but she couldn't. Besides, it was that constant accusation that had turned her mind to suspecting George Sawyer. And then she mentioned the mutual insurance policy.

"Everyone talked about how much the widow would gain, but

Mr. Sawyer will collect a million dollars in insurance money. Maybe more, given the way Mr. Collins died."

"Double indemnity."

"I guess."

She told the priest of the way both partners frequented the Rendezvous. "It was just outside that nightclub that Mr. Collins was struck. And by his own car, which was then left in the club parking lot where the police found it the next day."

"So your fear is that Mr. Sawyer, having taken the keys from your desk, used them to take his partner's car and run him down?"

"Yes."

"For the insurance money."

"Father, it's worse. I think he may have been responsible for the death of Bob Oliver as well."

"Good heavens."

She told him of George Sawyer's reaction to learning that Oliver and his photographer had been at the agency, of his strange behavior when he learned that the reporter had been in his partner's office.

"Was anything missing?"

"He didn't say that."

"Would you know if something was missing from Stanley Collins's office?"

Shirley stared at him. "I should have checked."

"Have you just come from the agency?"

"Yes."

"Would you like me to come back there with you while you see if anything is missing from Mr. Collins's office?"

"Would you?"

He rose. "It isn't just curiosity, Shirley. If there is any basis for your suspicions, it might not be safe for you to be there alone."

"Oh, my Lord."

It seemed to tell against her suspicion that she had never felt fear in the presence of George Sawyer.

Entering the office in the company of Father Dowling made it seem a strange place. The priest stood and looked about him.

"Show me where you kept the keys."

She took him to her desk and sat before opening the drawer. As she did so, she began again describing how she had done then just what she was doing now.

"I keep them all here, with little tags." She began to rummage through the keys in the plastic tray and then stopped.

"Is something the matter?"

For answer, Shirley held up a key. "This is it! It's back."

He sat across from her, and it helped that his reaction to her discovery was calm. Shirley's own mind was a cascade of thoughts.

"When did you last check the keys?"

"Father, he put it back here the other day. Now I am sure of it. He sat at this desk. I stepped out of the office, if only to get away from him. He was in a terrible mood. He was sitting here when I returned."

"And you're sure George Sawyer had it."

"What do you think?"

He had taken out his pipe and now seemed surprised to find it in his hand.

"I think you should call Lieutenant Horvath."

Cy Horvath went to the agency offices when he received Shirley Escalante's phone call and looked at the ignition key she took from the plastic tray in her desk drawer.

"This wasn't here when we looked before."

"No."

"What's the explanation?"

She observed a moment of silence, as if wondering what loyalty demanded. Then she said in a low voice, "Mr. Sawyer."

He listened while she told him of George Sawyer's coming to the office and sitting at her desk.

"There's more."

"Go on."

"He was very upset when I told him Bob Oliver had been here."

Her account of Oliver's visit, once alone, the second time with his photographer, was detailed.

"He was such a nice man."

For a moment he thought she meant George Sawyer.

"Have you any idea where George Sawyer is?"

"I could page him."

"Go ahead."

She left a message on Sawyer's pager, asking him to call in, not saying why. Ten minutes later the phone rang. It was Sawyer. Cy reached for the instrument.

"Sawyer? Lieutenant Horvath. Where can we meet?"

"Meet? What for?"

"I'd rather tell you personally."

"Lieutenant, I have to earn a living. I think you'll agree that I have been cooperative. Of course I'll see you again, but at the moment—"

"Where are you?"

A pause long enough to make Cy wonder if the connection had been broken. "As it happens, I am coming to the office."

"I'll be here."

From a window, Cy watched Sawyer pull into the parking lot behind the building. He sat in his car for a minute before the door opened and he got out, in shirtsleeves, swinging his suit jacket over his shoulder, an angry look on his face. He came through the door as if he were conducting a raid. He glared at Cy.

"Well, what is it?"

"Your partner's ignition key has turned up."

Sawyer assumed a look of disbelief. "What the hell difference does that make?"

"I'll explain it to you. Stanley Collins had been run over by his own car. His ignition key was in his pocket. There was no key in the car. So where was the key used by whoever ran down Collins?"

"His wife had a key. There was a key in the office." He looked at Shirley, who was standing next to her desk. "Show him the key to Stanley's car."

"This is it," Cy said, holding it up. "Miss Escalante just gave it to me."

"And that is why you wanted to talk to me?"

"The key has been missing, Sawyer. When I first came here to talk to Miss Escalante she told me about her tray of extra keys. The ignition key to Collins's car was missing. Now it's back."

Sawyer took a hanger from the coat rack and arranged his suit jacket on it and hung it up. He looked at Shirley. "Did you tell him about Bob Oliver's visit?"

"Yes."

Sawyer looked at Cy. "Does that help you?"

"How?"

"Oh, come on. Stanley was his brother-in-law. He hated his guts, and not without reason, considering the way he treated Oliver's sister."

"Phyllis."

"Phyllis."

"You think Bob Oliver killed his brother-in-law?"

"Horvath, you're the cop, not me. Figure it out."

"So who ran over Bob Oliver?"

"What are you talking about?"

"Haven't you heard?"

"Horvath, I don't know what in hell you are talking about."

Anyone who sold real estate had to be an actor of sorts. George Sawyer gave a convincing impression of someone who had not heard of the death of Bob Oliver. So Cy told him about it.

"I don't think he ran himself down, Sawyer. Any more than your partner did."

"Where did it happen?"

"Behind the Frosinone Hotel."

"The Frosinone! Maybe you better check with the Pianones."

"Maybe you better check with your lawyer."

"You're kidding."

"No. I am not kidding. Your lawyer would advise you to say

nothing while I point out to you that you and Stanley Collins were not on the best of terms. Quite apart from business difficulties, there was the matter of Wanda Janski. Stanley cut you out there, didn't he? Who better than you knew how he hung around the Rendezvous? You probably knew where he parked his car. And you knew where to get an ignition key."

His face assumed an expression of confused wonder. "We grew up together, we went to school together . . ." Sawyer's voice trailed off. All his blustering anger was gone. "Do you mean you're arresting me?"

"I am taking you in, yes. For questioning."

Sawyer had been standing during this exchange. Now he walked to Shirley's desk and picked up the phone. He looked at Cy. "I'm going to call my lawyer."

"Conflict of interest," Tuttle said. "I represent Phyllis Collins."

Tuttle was explaining why he hadn't been hired by George Sawyer. He and Peanuts had come to Cy's office where Cy was taking a break from talking to George Sawyer. Phil Keegan was with the Realtor and his lawyer, Murdstone. Presumably, Murdstone was advising Sawyer to keep his mouth shut. Tuttle had been in the press room when Cy brought George Sawyer in and for a wild moment thought he might pick up a quick client. But Sawyer brushed him off.

"I have a real lawyer."

"Well, you're in real estate."

Tuttle could count the times he had heard Cy Horvath laugh, and that was one of them. Cy had steered Sawyer down the hall and Tuttle followed close enough behind to have the door slammed in his face when the two men disappeared into a questioning room. Tuttle went back to the press room and woke up Peanuts.

"Get a car, Peanuts. They just pulled in George Sawyer."

If Peanuts had ever heard of the Realtor he gave no sign of it. But he went dutifully off to sign out a squad car. On the way to the Frosinone, he hit the siren a couple of times for the fun of it. Why were they going to the Frosinone? Because Tuttle assumed Sawyer was being questioned about the death of Bob Oliver. Out of family loyalty, Peanuts parked the squad car behind the hotel, and they entered through the door left open so that the men working on the elevators could come and go. They found Primo in the dining room with a pot of tea and a plate of toast in front of him. Tuttle pulled up a chair, and Peanuts followed suit.

Tuttle said, "I don't have to tell you who Peanuts represents." He let the thought establish itself in Primo's mind. "The Frosinone is getting all the wrong kind of publicity."

"Bob Oliver," Primo groaned.

"May he rest in peace."

The sentiment surprised Primo. "Yeah. Right."

"Lucky for you the cops have a lead."

"Who?"

"What do you know of George Sawyer?"

"George Sawyer? Who's he?"

"The man being questioned about Bob Oliver's death in the alley behind this hotel."

"It's a public alley."

"You're probably next on the list, Primo."

"What list?"

"I am surprised the police haven't been here already."

"Been here? Of course they've been here. I told them all I know, which is nothing."

"You told them about Oliver and Flora?"

Primo pushed back from the table and started to rise, but Peanuts put a hand on his shoulder and held him down. As if on cue, Flora appeared in the entrance of the dining room. She ran across the room to Primo.

"Don't tell them!"

"Sit down, Flora," Tuttle said. Peanuts brought up a chair and looked as if he might put her in it. She sat.

"Did you?" she asked Primo.

"Shut up, Flora. Okay?"

She relaxed. "So you didn't. Good. I don't want to be involved."

Tuttle tipped back his tweed hat and assumed a look of understanding. "I know how you must feel."

"I don't even know who he was, and I don't want to know."

"He asked you about Bob Oliver?"

The hunch floated down from above, like an inspiration from Tuttle senior, up there in the sky, strumming on a harp.

"Shut up, Flora."

"Stop telling me to shut up."

"I will if you shut up."

"Tell me about it," Tuttle said gently. "It will all come out eventually, you know."

"There's nothing to come out."

"Nothing that can harm you, I'm sure."

"I thought he was with the work crew. You know, the boss or something."

"How would you describe him?"

"I wouldn't. He wore a suit."

"Let me give you a description." And Tuttle drew a little word picture of George Sawyer. Flora's reaction told him his father was still at work.

"They have him downtown right now for questioning, Flora. Your placing him at the Frosinone could be important." Tuttle turned to Primo. "Did you see George Sawyer here that day?"

"I told you I don't know George Sawyer."

"The man I described."

"It was that same day," Flora said. "The day they found Bob in the alley."

Primo said to Peanuts, "I thought you represented the family. Say something."

"Shut up," Peanuts said.

"Let him talk," Tuttle said.

"I've got nothing to say."

"He's jealous," Flora said, with a contemptuous laugh. "A man walks in here and the first thing he thinks is . . ."

"Just like with Bob Oliver?"

"Yes!"

"Primo," Tuttle said. "The way I see it, you're in big trouble. Anyone who has ever been in this hotel knows how jealous you are about Flora. Naturally the cops are going to wonder if you did something about it."

Primo laughed. "I already told the cops, Tuttle. I don't drive. I never have. I don't know how."

"That could help."

"Help? I don't need any help."

"Primo, you need legal help. I am not soliciting business. It is simply good professional advice."

"Send me a bill."

"Do you want representation?"

"Sure, represent me."

"Give me a dollar."

"A dollar? What for?"

"That way you engage me as your lawyer."

Flora opened a purse the size of a mailbag and took out a wallet. She sailed a dollar bill across the table.

Tuttle said, "Hand it to me, Primo."

Primo looked at the crumpled bill lying beside his plate of toast. He reached out, picked it up like the claw in a gumball machine, and handed it to Tuttle. Tuttle swept off his hat and put the dollar in the crown, among his business cards. He gave one of the cards to Primo.

"Smart move. So let me go over what we know. George Sawyer had come to the Frosinone. Flora had spotted him standing in the open door and went to see what he wanted."

Primo growled to Flora, "Is that your idea of being retired?"

"You'll drive me back into the life, Primo. Honest to God you will."

"I don't drive."

Peanuts snickered. Tuttle went on. Sawyer had come to make inquiries about Bob Oliver. He had a photograph of the journalist. Of course, Flora knew who he was. And she told him, sure, Oliver liked to drink in the bar of the Frosinone.

"I thought he was someone's husband, you know. Mad."

"Okay," Tuttle said. "We got motive, we got opportunity, we got George Sawyer at the Frosinone an hour before Oliver got nailed." He stood and looked at Primo.

"This should get you off the hook, Primo. But if the cops come, you call me right away. I'll be in touch. Come on, Peanuts."

They used the siren all the way back to the courthouse.

8

Father Dowling learned of the effect of Shirley Escalante's call to
the police from Phil Keegan when he stopped by the rectory.
Phil had a look that mingled satisfaction with irritation.

"Of course Murdstone won't let him answer any questions."

"You think he killed them both?"

Phil laughed. "What I think or don't think doesn't matter. The
case against him is strong. He won't talk, and when he goes to trial
Murdstone will plead him not guilty. If he ever speaks of it later,
he will deny it. If it were just a matter of thinking, there are always
two sides, even if one side is a lie. The prosecutor isn't interested
in what I think or in what Cy thinks but in what a jury will have to
think when he lays it all out for him. The fact that he was asking
about Oliver around the Frosinone would have clinched it."

"Would have?"

"There is physical evidence that he was in the cab of that
truck. We found some fingerprints of his in Collins's car, but it
wouldn't take a Murdstone to explain those away. After all, the
men were partners. But he left his handkerchief in the pickup
that ran down Oliver."

"His handkerchief!"

"He must have used it to wipe down the steering wheel, the shift, the door handle. No fingerprints at all."

"And what will Murdstone say to that?"

"Oh, there's more. There were some moccasins hidden away in the back of a drawer in his desk. They match imprints on the floor of the truck's cab."

"Good Lord."

Phil nodded and sipped his beer. "So it's all wrapped up."

"You don't seem too happy."

"Prison will be especially hard for a man like Sawyer."

"His motives seem murky enough."

"Oh, I don't know. In the case of Stanley Collins it was money. And revenge, of a sort."

"But why Bob Oliver?"

"Motive matters less there, given what we've found. I suppose he feared that Oliver had found him out."

"Do you suppose Oliver ever really intended to write a feature about the agency?"

"Who knows? Now he could write one about two merry widows. The partners are out of the picture but their wives are sitting pretty."

"I don't think Phyllis Collins thinks of herself as a merry widow."

Marie Murkin looked in, no merry widow she, and looked from Father Dowling to Phil. "You two look glum enough."

"Bring me another beer to brighten me up."

"Only if you tell me all about George Sawyer."

Father Dowling listened to another recitation of the facts in the case. They seemed more damning when heard a second time. Marie, at least, showed satisfaction in the outcome. But she rejected the theory of the merry widows.

"Maybe Susan Sawyer. But not Mrs. Collins. The Sawyers

234   Ralph McInerny

were married in the Church. The other woman will be no sort of widow at all."

"Now Marie, don't turn that into an argument for capital punishment."

"Oh, I know you would let him off with a scolding. And a penance. Maybe three Hail Marys."   /

Marie had an exaggerated opinion of his capacity for mercy, Father Dowling thought after Phil had left and the housekeeper had climbed the back stairway to her room. Alone in his study, he recalled Stanley Collins's visit, followed by that of his wife. David Jameson's ardor had cooled in the meantime, or rather been redirected toward Bridget, his nurse. Would the two of them go on working together, bestowing the smiles that nature had failed to give?

When Edna had told him of the arrangements she had made to have women from the senior center take turns spending time with Phyllis Collins, Father Dowling had dropped by to find the widow alone.

"I thought someone would be with you."

"Please, the thought of another sympathetic old woman gives me the willies. I have never felt so commiserated over, not even at the wake and funeral. Of course, I know what brings them. David Jameson actually sent his nurse to look after me."

"Bridget."

"She never liked me. I'm sure she turned him against me."

"So it's all over."

"It never was much." She tossed her head. The coloring of her hair had dimmed and there were silver threads among the artful gold.

"Was there only your brother?"

She nodded and gave a little sob. "Poor Bob. And he was so pleased that I had come into so much money."

"No other relatives?"

She shook her head. "Susan Sawyer says we should go on a cruise together. Maybe we will. You would think what's happened would have driven us apart, but we're becoming great friends."

Brochures advertising Caribbean cruises and round-the-world voyages arrived even at the St. Hilary rectory. Marie professed to be surprised by this but the brochures seemed to disappear, doubtless going up the back stairs to Marie's room. Did she moon over them, seeing herself on shipboard in the moonlight?

"Lots of people go on cruises," Marie said, when he teased her about it.

"In your case it seems almost inevitable."

"What do you mean?"

"You were married to a sailor, after all."

He hadn't meant to be cruel, but the reminder of her late husband sent Marie into several days of uncharacteristic mourning. She seldom had a good word to say of the man who had married her and then abandoned her, returning as an old man to make a definitive widow of her. Well, sorrow need not be logical. Father Dowling told Marie he would say a Mass for her husband.

"Oh, do. I pray for him every day, Father."

"Good for you."

"He needs all the prayers he can get."

"We all do."

Marie seemed ready to argue the point, but he left her to her memories. In the mood she was in, it was just as well that he was dining out with Amos Cadbury. Ordinarily, Marie would have loved to prepare a meal for the lawyer, but in her current lugubrious mood she did not even complain when he said that he and Amos would be eating at the University Club.

Amos Cadbury liked an early dinner and he expected Father Dowling at six, but already at five-thirty the lawyer was ensconced in the club library, a Manhattan at his elbow and an open volume of Dickens ignored on his lap. Long thoughts came to him in the waning light of day. He had spent the afternoon putting the final touches on old Frederick Collins's will. How oddly awry go the plans of men. One did not have to be a lawyer to be struck by this, but in recent years Amos had spent much of his time probating the wills of departed clients and insuring that their money went where they had wished it. As often as not, this required him to occupy the spirit of a will, its letter being no longer possible of realization. Oh, he could tell tales of people who were meant to receive handsome bequests who had passed away before the person who bequeathed them. But Frederick Collins's will was particularly poignant.

Married late, Frederick and his wife had spoiled Stanley, their only child, and then tried to lessen the effects of this in the will they had made. Stanley would be a rich man, but not yet. He had proved himself capable of such folly that postponement seemed the prudent course. Not that Amos had not been surprised by the plan to make Stanley an heir when he turned fifty. That was a birthday Stanley was destined never to see. For years he had accepted the terms of the will until, stimulated by the bad advice of the ineffable Tuttle, he had sought to lay hands on the money that was coming to him. This was a struggle Amos had expected soon after the demise of the parents, but Stanley had accepted the terms for years. Now all that money would go to the daughter-in-law the senior Collinses had never known.

One of the oddest events of recent months had been the visit to his office by Phyllis Collins and Dr. David Jameson. Amos had not led an entirely sheltered life, but the brazenness of Mrs. Collins, bringing her altogether too attentive dentist to discover what divorce and remarriage would do to her prospects of sharing in Stanley's inheritance, had impressed him. But then Amos regarded the pleasure he had taken in dashing her hopes as a confessable fault. He said as much to Father Dowling when he arrived and they were settled at a table with a delightful view of the lake through the window beside them.

"Marie called them the odd couple."

"I would not have thought Dr. Jameson would be smitten by such a woman."

"The infatuation has run its course, apparently."

"So he wasn't after her money. Now there is money to be had, a great deal of money. I hope to convince her to use it wisely."

"She mentioned going on a cruise."

Amos sighed. "Of course."

"The suggestion came from Mrs. Sawyer."

"Her I have not met." It might have been an expression of thanksgiving.

"Amos, when I was a student we studied the arguments of St. Thomas Aquinas on false candidates for happiness. Money was one of them."

"How did the argument run?"

Father Dowling summarized as best he could what the saint had said. "But he added something to the arguments against wealth and pleasure and fame constituting happiness. He said the best proof against them is having them."

"Ah, that is an argument I can heartily endorse. I fear that wealth will prove a mixed blessing for Mrs. Collins as it has for so many others."

"You must give me a lawyer's view of the case against George Sawyer."

"Murdstone is no Tuttle, but even so, there is little he will be able to do to save his client from conviction. The physical evidence, as I have heard it, is decisive."

"I sometimes think it is easier to imagine those we do not know as guilty. I have never met George Sawyer."

"Nor I. But he will be on everyone's lips while the trial goes on. Did you know that convicts keep scrapbooks of the media coverage of their trials?"

"A brief hour in the sun of public attention."

"Is that from St. Thomas?"

"He wasn't given to metaphors."

"I am sure that Dr. Jameson did not enjoy it when he was under suspicion."

"He is a very earnest man."

"What he does is a species of cosmetic surgery, isn't it?"

"'Everyone has a natural right to a perfect smile.' That isn't Aquinas either."

Amos smiled. "It is a temptation, I know, but sometimes like Mr. Bennet in *Pride and Prejudice,* I think that others have been put on earth to keep us bemused. But then Mr. Bennet bemuses me, too."

"I may visit George Sawyer."

"Is he a Catholic?"

"Marie assures me they were married in the Church. And haven't been in one since."

"He may find the consolations of religion attractive now."

When George Sawyer was brought into the visiting room he stopped and stared at Father Dowling, then turned to leave but the guard stood in his way.

"I don't want to see a priest."

"I was told you're a Catholic."

A wry smile came over Sawyer's face. "Well, I was."

"You don't have to talk with me if you don't want to."

"Who sent you?"

"Oh, I am here entirely on my own." Father Dowling took out his pipe and began to fill it. Sawyer moved toward a chair and sat. He took out a package of cigarettes.

"I've taken up smoking again. What difference does it make?"

"Well, I wouldn't recommend it as a means of suicide. Smoking has more positive benefits."

"You did the funeral for Stanley Collins."

"Of course. You were there."

"Of course." He repeated it in a sarcastic tone. "I'm sorry. You have to realize that I had known Stanley all my life. We went to school together, we were in college together. Marquette."

"Ah, the Jesuits."

"Later we went into business together. Of course, we fought like cats and dogs. I should say like old friends. Now they accuse me of killing him."

"Things look bad for you."

"Don't I know it. Not even my lawyer pretends I have a Chinaman's chance." He looked over both shoulders. "Can I still say that? Where I'm going I'll have to be careful what I say."

Father Dowling thought of telling him he knew the chaplain at Joliet, but that seemed an odd way to comfort the man.

"You sound resigned."

"Explain providence to me, Father. Or fate. Whatever it is that makes a joke of life." He puffed on his cigarette, then studied its glowing end. "Take smoking. I had an uncle who died of lung cancer. Never smoked in his life."

"You should complain to the surgeon general."

Sawyer laughed joylessly. "Stanley and I used to compose letters to the editor. We never sent them, but it was great fun." His eyes drifted away. "Sometimes I think I saw all this coming."

"All what?"

"Do you know of Stanley's inheritance? All his life he looked forward to turning fifty when he would be rich. Now that looks like a joke played on him. I wonder where I'll be when I turn fifty." He put out his cigarette and shook another from the package.

"So you are Catholic?"

"Oh, sure. Does anyone ever stop? You stop going to church and all the rest, but if I filled out a form I would write Catholic. The way I would write Irish."

"It goes a little deeper than that."

Sawyer had lit the fresh cigarette. "Did you come to hear my confession?"

"Well, I am a priest."

"It's funny. They use the same word here. Confession. They expect me to make a confession."

"The other kind is more important."

"Father, I didn't kill anybody." He peered at Father Dowling. "Of course, you expect me to say that. My plea will be not guilty, but that's only a legal formality for Murdstone. He thinks I'm guilty."

"But you're not?"

"Oh, I'm guilty of lots of things. The whole book, probably."

"So get it off your chest."

"I thought sin was on the soul."

"Then get it off your soul."

"Even my wife thinks I'm guilty. I mean of killing Stanley and that other guy."

"Has she said so?"

"You've heard of body language. I know what she thinks."

"Maybe I should talk with her, too."

"We were married in the Church. A beautiful ceremony in Wauwatosa. Stanley was my best man. He got married in front of a judge."

"He came to see me."

"Stanley?"

"And his wife."

"Were they going to get their marriage blessed at last?"

"Did he ever mention that to you?"

"It was his favorite subject. His claim was that he wasn't really married to Phyllis so playing around wasn't all that bad. If he got a divorce it didn't mean anything because he wasn't married in the first place. Is that true?"

"It's a little more complicated than that."

"He talked of marrying Wanda Janski." Sawyer looked wistful. "She's a singer."

"I've met her."

"In daylight? You had to hear her sing to understand. The joke is I introduced Stanley to her."

Father Dowling stayed for nearly an hour, and when he left asked George Sawyer if he would like him to come back.

"If you want. I don't like to have Susan come here. Did you mean that about talking to her?"

"Would you advise it?"

Sawyer shrugged. "What could it hurt? Maybe you can convince her I didn't kill Stanley."

Susan Sawyer agreed to see him with some reluctance. The fact that he had visited George seemed to be in his favor. They met at a fast-food place in the mall over coffee.

"I can't remember the last time I talked with a priest."

"Not many people make a diary entry when they do."

She smiled, if only at the effort to make a joke. "It's not as if I lost my faith. I am deeply into spirituality."

"Tell me about it."

She cocked her head to one side. "Are you making fun of me?"

"God forbid."

"People laugh about New Age spirituality but that's because they don't understand it. George pooh-poohed it, of course."

"Of course."

"He claims to be an agnostic."

"That's not much help to him at the moment."

"I have talked with his lawyer, Father. Miles Murdstone. Everything seems as certain as it can be. I tell myself George could not have done these things. I cannot imagine him killing anyone, let alone Stanley Collins."

"He says he didn't."

"I know." Silence. "I think he's following his lawyer's instructions."

"You think he did it?"

"I'll tell you a secret. I don't want to think about it. I'm sick and tired of thinking about it. I have to think of what I will do now."

"I talked with Phyllis Collins."

"This has drawn the two of us closer than we've ever been. Isn't that odd? We haven't been able to stand one another for years, and now we practically cling to one another. What has happened has happened, and we have to go on, somehow."

She seemed to have consigned her husband to his fate and was determined not to be undone herself by what had happened to him. Of course, her husband was now branded as the murderer of two men and that would considerably alter her attitude toward him.

"How long have you been married?"

"Fifteen years."

That was all. He let it go. Father Dowling found Susan Sawyer inscrutable.

The next time he visited George Sawyer, they talked about the evidence that had been gathered against him. Despite that, he said again that he was innocent. And so it might have remained if George Sawyer had not said, "Last time you talked about going to confession."

"Would you like to?"

"Here?"

"Why not? It's as private as any confessional." He took the stole from his jacket pocket, turned it to its purple side, and put it on.

"I don't know where to begin."

"Why don't I just run through things, the large sins, and you can respond."

And so they went through pride and theft and adultery and other sins of the flesh, all the capital sins but one. George accused himself of breaking every commandment mentioned.

"Anything else?"

"That's all the big ones."

There had been no mention of murder.

"Sure?"

George Sawyer nodded. As he recited the formula of absolution, making the sign of the cross over the penitent, Father Dowling told himself that Sawyer would not have held back anything, given what he had confessed.

"So that's that."

"I feel lighter."

"Don't wait so long next time."

"I wonder where next time will be."

Marie Murkin did not conceal her satisfaction that justice would be done. The fact that George Sawyer was accused of killing a man who had visited the rectory made it seem almost a personal affront.

"They should lock him up and throw away the key."

Phil put down his beer. "Punishment isn't what it was, Marie."

"I know. I have no doubt he will be walking free in a few years, and yet those two men will still be dead."

That afternoon, Father Dowling had gone over to the school and talked with Edna Hospers.

"Many women are sorry we've stopped them from taking turns spending time with Phyllis Collins, but she has come out of the doldrums. Mrs. Sawyer is so wonderful. She spends so much time with her that there is no longer any reason to ask for volunteers. But the women miss it."

"Have you yourself been there?"

Edna nodded. "That's what caused me to call off the visitations. Nice as it was of the old ladies, I think they were becoming a nuisance. Besides, Phyllis is seldom alone now. Susan Sawyer sees to that."

"Birds of a feather."

"Oh, but they aren't. Phyllis is such a chucklehead. Susan will be a very good influence on her."

"Are they still talking about going on a cruise?"

"They have all kinds of literature they're poring over. I told them it was a great idea." Edna paused. "It wasn't a great idea suggesting to Susan that she and I had things in common. I mentioned that Earl had spent time in prison, and she just cut me off. I thought I could say things that would be of help to her, but she wasn't interested. You would think that *she* was the widow rather than Phyllis. Well, that is how some people cope with it. I gather it wasn't too happy a marriage."

"Apparently not."

"Earl said that once he gets into prison he will be with people who did far worse things."

But Father Dowling had come to think that George Sawyer was as innocent as he claimed to be. He could not believe that the man would have gone through the humiliation of that long confession and left out the reason he was sitting in jail. Under the circumstances, confessing murder would have been relatively easy. But that left all the material evidence against George unexplained. He had left his handkerchief in the cab of the truck and the imprint of his office moccasins had been found on the floorboard. He had been asking about Bob Oliver around the Frosinone and learned that he was often there. And there was the less conclusive link of the ignition key of Stanley's car, gone from the tray in Shirley Escalante's desk and then mysteriously returned after George had been sitting in her chair. George Sawyer had no explanation for any of that. When Father Dowling had reviewed the evidence, he looked away, his expression desolate, his mouth a thin line.

When Marie and Phil talked about the case, Father Dowling could no longer take part, and it was an effort not to call attention to the fact that he was not chiming in. Marie, of course, noticed.

"I know what you're thinking. They're just sins, and sins can be forgiven, and that ought to be enough."

"Is that what I'm thinking, Marie?"

"You probably think that Judas repented even while he was hanging himself."

"I had no idea you were a mind reader."

"Some minds are easy to read."

But no mind can be read, not really. Each of us is a mystery to himself and even more so to others. Much as he wanted to be certain that George Sawyer's failure to confess the crimes for which he was being held was proof of innocence, he could not exclude the possibility that George had made a bad confession and received an absolution that was ineffective because he had concealed mortal sins.

The following day Shirley Escalante came to the rectory. Marie brought her to the study and left her there, obviously having failed to find out the purpose of the visit. When the door closed, Shirley began to cry.

"Oh, Father, I feel so awful. If I hadn't told the police about that key . . ."

"I advised you to do that, Shirley."

"I know, I know. But I feel that I'm the one who put him jail."

"You know better than that. I am told that he will be tried for the murder of Bob Oliver first, and there may be no reason to try him for Stanley Collins's death."

"But I told them his reaction to Bob Oliver's visit to the office. That is why they began to make inquiries at that hotel. And then they came and found those moccasins in his office."

"And his handkerchief in the truck."

Shirley took a deep breath. "Even so, I just cannot believe he did such a thing. When he and Mr. Collins quarreled, I always took Mr. Collins's side, if only in my own mind, but George Sawyer was in his way a good man. Mrs. Sawyer was as upset about Bob Oliver's visit as she was."

"Mrs. Sawyer?"

"She stopped by the office that same day."

"Did the Sawyers leave together?"

"No, she had already left."

"And the key was back in your drawer."

"I didn't know that right away."

"What did she say about Bob Oliver?"

"Oh, she wanted to know what he had done while he was there. She seemed angry that I had let him look in the offices. She went into her husband's and shut the door. Brooding, I suppose. What difference did it make that a reporter had been there and taken photographs? I was glad when she finally left."

"What time was that."

Shirley thought. "Four? When did you come?"

"Before five. Four-thirty, probably."

"And that's when I found the key."

"Let's review that whole afternoon, Shirley."

He made a little chronology as she reconstructed it, Susan letting herself in at four, George coming after four, Father Dowling coming after he left.

"She let herself in?"

"She seemed to think the office would be empty."

"I suppose it isn't surprising that she would have a key to the office."

"She worked there, before I came."

Hazel was in seventh heaven when she heard of the money Phyllis Collins would now have, and Tuttle did not cast a cloud over her assumption that he had triumphed unequivocally. Oh, there was a check, a very large check, but it represented all he would ever see of the money that had finally come to the widow Collins. His wild dream of being put in control of her money was dashed during the first moments in Amos Cadbury's office. The amount of her monthly stipend brought a little gasp from Phyllis Collins.

"I have invested the money over the years, Mrs. Collins, and I would advise you to simply leave it as it is."

Cadbury handed Phyllis a sheet on which was recorded the initial amount set aside for Stanley Collins and how it had grown in the intervening years. Reading it over her shoulder, Tuttle could have wept. Of course, Cadbury had papers prepared, and Tuttle knew better than to suggest that she not sign them, or at least take them home to study them. The monthly income that was now hers had completely bedazzled her. Tuttle could hardly blame her.

Throughout the meeting, Amos Cadbury more or less ignored Tuttle's presence. But then he produced a check for Phyllis to sign, made out to Tuttle. She scrawled her signature on it as Tuttle's eyes rounded at the amount. Cadbury put the check in an envelope and handed it to Tuttle. And then they actually shook hands.

"I think you will agree that things have turned out well for Mrs. Collins."

Tuttle agreed.

He went down in the elevator with Phyllis Collins, listening to her sing the praises of Amos Cadbury. She seemed to think that the lawyer had made her a present of all that money. Tuttle put his hand on his chest in order to feel the reassuring crinkle of the check in his pocket. This was the check that Hazel now regarded as if it were a sacred object.

"I'm going to get this into the bank pronto."

"Good idea."

"Are you still her lawyer?"

"I've done what she hired me to do."

"Good man." Tuttle ducked out of range as she tried to kiss his cheek. She left for the bank, singing "Anchors Aweigh." Tuttle went into his office, closed the door, got settled behind his desk, and sought the comforting darkness of his lowered tweed hat. How sweetly sad was success. He had not known much of it, but the few times luck had turned his way had been oddly disappointing. He shook away such melancholy thoughts in order to commune with his departed father.

But the uncustomary meditative mood persisted as his thoughts shifted to George Sawyer. An indictment for the murder of Bob Oliver had been brought in, Murdstone had pleaded his client not guilty, no surprise there. Tuttle pushed back his hat, feeling once more the twitch of avarice. Inspiration had struck. He scrambled out of his chair and hurried from the office. On the stairs, he told himself that there was no way Hazel could have finished at the bank and be returning, still it was with genuine relief that he slid behind the wheel of his car. He was about to turn the key when a noise in the back seat caused him to freeze. He turned slowly to find Peanuts sleeping in the back seat. No need to wake him. He started the car on the second try and headed for the Frosinone.

When he parked in the alley behind the hotel, Peanuts did not waken, and Tuttle left him in repose as he went through the open door used by the crew still working on the elevators. Before entering the lobby, he looked around the elevators to see if Primo Verdi was on duty. He was. Was this good or bad? Well, he'd find out.

"Want to register, Tuttle?" Verdi said.

"I never vote. Is Flora around?"

Verdi closed his eyes and groaned. "I wish she weren't."

"I want to talk with her."

"Good, take her away. She's driving me nuts."

"How so?"

"She's been subpoenaed to testify in George Sawyer's trial."

"Just why I'm here."

Verdi was already busy on the phone. He held the receiver to his ear and looked abstractedly across the lobby.

"Flora? Tuttle, the lawyer, is coming up."

He immediately put down the phone. "Two nineteen."

"Second floor?"

Verdi just looked at him. Tuttle headed for the stairway, a beautiful ornate stairway rising in a gentle curve under a massive chandelier.

A head appeared as he approached the door of 219, looked first away and then toward Tuttle. He got to the door before she could close it.

"We have to talk about your testimony."

"Go away. I won't testify. I'll tell them I'm sick."

Tuttle nodded. "No, I will tell them. Let's talk it out."

She stopped pushing on the door, and he let himself in. He looked around the suite, showing approval.

"Much better than a jail cell."

"Jail cell!"

"Well, let's not talk of that yet. It's where you'll end up if you refuse to honor a subpoena."

She began to wail, but this caused no consternation in Tuttle. Dealing with Hazel had diminished his fear of the female of the species. He let her wail for a few minutes. When she tired of it, he began again.

"We have to run through the questions that will be put to you on the stand."

"I haven't given you a dollar."

"You're right. Give me a dollar."

She hesitated and then went for her purse. She handed Tuttle a dollar. "Primo says you're worth every penny of that."

Tuttle shook his head. "A bitter man. Now then. In your own words, tell me about George Sawyer's asking you about Bob Oliver."

"That's all there is. He asked me if I knew Bob Oliver."

"And you said yes."

"I thought it was a referral. Don't tell Primo that."

"Our conversation is protected by the lawyer-client privilege. Think of me as a priest."

She laughed. "What religion?"

"But it wasn't a referral?"

"No. He wanted to talk about Bob Oliver."

"How did he act? Angry?"

"Oh, no. He wanted to know if anyone else had been looking for Oliver."

"Did he say who?"

Flora made a face, indicative of thought. "I got the impression that it was a woman. Maybe he was an angry husband. Not that he acted angry."

Tuttle led her through as complete a recall of her conversation with George Sawyer as she could muster.

"That wasn't so bad, was it?"

"I still want to call in sick."

Tuttle had been folding the dollar bill she gave him and it had taken the form of a paper plane. Not that he thought it would fly.

When he went out to his car, he stood in the alley, wondering why Flora had gotten the impression that George Sawyer was a wronged husband. He pulled open the door of his car, got in, and was nearly frightened out of his wits by the awakening Peanuts.

"Good Lord. I forgot all about you."

"Where are we?"

"On our way to dinner."

As they ate at the Great Wall of China, Tuttle explored with Peanuts the possibility that there was something wrong with the Sawyer marriage. After all, the Collins marriage had been a mess. Peanuts nodded through it all, not really listening.

"I'll have to look into it," he said to Peanuts.

"What?"

13

One of the charms of the priesthood, Amos Cadbury had always thought, is its reminder that sins can be forgiven. Saints develop a conscience so sensitive that it would strike the average person as scrupulous, but Amos took that as proof that the remission of sin did not coarsen one's sense of good and evil. Such thoughts occurred when Father Dowling enlisted his aid.

"I could not myself hire an investigator, Amos. The truth is I feel sheepish asking you to do so. But George Sawyer's persistence in claiming his innocence raises the possibility that someone else is guilty of the crimes he is charged with."

"A plea of not guilty is not really a claim of innocence, Father."

"Captain Keegan assures me that Sawyer does claim to be innocent."

Father Dowling must know that most criminals claim to be innocent, but Amos felt inclined to indulge his old friend. It seemed right that a priest should give credence even to so incredible a claim as Sawyer's.

"So what would you want an investigator to do?"

"If I knew, I wouldn't need one."

What Amos instructed Aloysius Parker to do when he hired

him was to look into every aspect of the evidence against George Sawyer. It was thus that he learned of the testimony that Flora was expected to make against George Sawyer.

"There's no doubt that he was at the Frosinone asking about Oliver."

Whenever Parker spoke he acted as if he were reading from the notebook he held open in his hand.

"You talked with Flora?"

Parker turned a page and nodded. "Say he wasn't asking for the reason the prosecutor will try to establish. Why else would he be asking about Oliver?"

Flora had told Parker that her first impression was that Sawyer was an irate husband, and that was the spoor he pursued. He had turned up some lurid facts, if they were facts, about Mrs. Sawyer. Wanda Janski told him that Stanley Collins had said to her that he once had a fling with his partner's wife. But it was Sylvia the photographer who linked Bob Oliver and Susan Sawyer. Literally, in a photograph.

"This was taken last year. He doesn't look too enthusiastic, does he?"

The photograph had been taken on the street, outside a building in which Oliver had been researching a feature. When they exited the building, the woman was waiting for Oliver. In the photograph he seemed more embraced than embracing. Sylvia had finished up a film with shots of Oliver and the woman.

"When I teased him about it, he just called her an old flame. So I went to the archives and matched the picture I had taken."

The woman was Susan Sawyer.

*   *   *

When Amos summarized Parker's report for Father Dowling, he emphasized that none of it was of much help to George Sawyer. Parker had simply turned up further proof of the fragility of human nature, and neither Father Dowling nor the courts were in need of that.

"I did pass it on to Murdstone, for what it is worth."

"Poor Parker," Father Dowling said. "What a way to make a living."

The trial of George Sawyer for the murder of Bob Oliver opened with several days devoted to the boring process of jury selection. Murdstone, advised by psychologists, palmologists, and psychics, sought to put in the jury box men and women suspicious of logic and sequential reasoning. Father Dowling looked in on both days. Susan Sawyer sat conspicuously behind her accused husband. On the second day, Father Dowling waited for her in the corridor outside the courtroom.

"Mrs. Sawyer," he called, and she turned. She began to smile but settled for a frown.

"I wonder if we could talk."

She settled herself where she stood. "Yes?"

"I didn't mean here. Would you care for coffee?"

"At the moment I would like something stronger."

So it was that Father Dowling found himself in the sports bar across from the courthouse, sipping his coffee while Susan Sawyer drank half her martini on the first try. She put the glass on the table and sighed.

"I thought that session would never end."

"It is good of you to attend."

"Murdstone insists on it, for whatever good it does. George has stopped speaking. I think he has decided to withdraw into himself. A kind of autism."

"What must it be like to be put on trial if you really are innocent of the charge?"

"His plea is not guilty, of course."

"With all that evidence against him, it does seem hopeless."

"Oh, they wouldn't let him plead guilty."

"Are you serious that he won't speak to you?"

"Father, I don't blame him. He is like a cornered animal."

"Do you think that he killed Bob Oliver?"

She drank some more. "Father, we went through this before. It doesn't matter what I think."

"How well did you know Bob Oliver?'

She tucked in her chin and looked at him over her glasses. "How well?"

"His photographer took this picture of you with him." He slid a large black-and-white photo from the manila envelope he had brought. Susan stared at it.

"I don't know anything about that picture." She peered at it as if unsure she was the woman embracing Bob Oliver.

"Apparently the photographer took these just to finish up a roll. There are six or eight of them in all."

"Why did she give them to you?"

"She didn't. They are the fruit of a series of inquiries."

"Inquiries about what?"

Father Dowling turned his coffee mug ninety degrees. "If your husband is accused of killing Bob Oliver, some motive has to be provided."

"Motive? He was mad at him for snooping around the agency offices."

"That angered you, too, didn't it?"

"Of course it did. How would you like someone invading your rectory and snooping around, taking pictures?" She glanced at the photograph before her.

"Shirley told me how upset you were."

"Shirley!"

Father Dowling nodded. "What I've tried to do is imagine some other explanation for all the damning evidence against your husband. Someone goes to the agency and returns the key used to start Stanley Collins's car. Later that same person will return the moccasins borrowed from your husband's office on the same occasion. The moccasins that left their imprint on the floor of the truck."

"And who would that someone be?"

"She would have to have access to his handkerchiefs, of course."

" 'She'?"

"Would you like another of those?"

"I'm fine. Thank you."

"I can understand how, out of passion, you would have run down Bob Oliver, but to incriminate your husband . . ."

In the noisy bar they might have been talking of anything. Susan straightened in her chair.

"I hope you don't intend to tell anyone that fantastic story."

"Your fingerprints on the ignition key would not prove much, perhaps. Or even one or two in Stanley's car. But in the cab of the truck . . ."

"There weren't any fingerprints."

"Because you had wiped them away."

"Are you actually accusing me of killing Bob Oliver?"

We cannot read the minds of others, but the eyes have been called the windows of the soul. Father Dowling had a brief glimpse of the tortured soul of Susan Sawyer.

"Yes, I am. And Stanley Collins, too. The question is, what are you going to do about it?"

After a moment she stood and looked down at him, her expression calm but icy.

"Thank you for the martini."

He rose, and together they left the bar.

"Can I give you a lift?"

"I have my car."

Parked across the street as was his. Traffic came in bursts, in response to the change of the traffic light at the corner to their left. While they waited, Father Dowling was filled with a sense of futility. His hunch had turned up the photograph linking Susan Sawyer to the unfortunate Bob Oliver, but he had played that card and been trumped by her cool dismissal of it. But, of course, a woman capable of what he was now certain she had done would be prepared to brazen out his accusation.

"You can't let someone else suffer for your sins."

She turned and looked at him scornfully. "I thought that was the whole idea."

She turned away and stepped into the street in what seemed a lull in the traffic. Suddenly a car that had rounded the corner on the red light accelerated to make the green at the next corner. Father Dowling grabbed Susan Sawyer's arm and pulled her out of harm's way. The car came to a stop where she had been. She turned to him ashen faced and came trembling into his arms. The sound of the braking car caused her to unravel, and what he had said in the bar had its belated effect. She looked at him, a woman no longer able to conceal the dreadful things she had done. When she stepped back from him, he said, "Why don't we have a talk with Lieutenant Horvath?"

She bit her lip, but her recent escape from the fate she had contrived for Stanley and Bob Oliver overcame her. It must have struck her as a quasi-divine judgment on what she had done. She nodded and turned away. He took her arm and led her safely across the street.

When Father Dowling ushered Susan Sawyer into Cy's office she immediately slumped into a chair.

"Mrs. Sawyer has something to say to you, Cy."

Cy took the envelope the priest gave him.

"It's a photograph. She'll explain."

Cy looked at the photograph of Susan Sawyer and Bob Oliver and immediately realized its significance, helped by Mrs. Sawyer's defeated expression.

"She's had a harrowing experience."

"I could have been run over . . ." Her voice trailed off.

"Tell me about it."

She began to speak in a dull voice, putting recent events in a new and intelligible light. Father Dowling took advantage of a pause to say he would leave them now.

"We can talk again later," he said to Mrs. Sawyer.

She nodded. She seemed reluctant to have Father Dowling leave. So was Cy, in a way, but now was the moment of justice. Mercy could wait. He felt a bit like a priest himself as he listened to her half-hysterical confession.

Susan Sawyer's confession prompted Zola to postpone the trial of George Sawyer and Murdstone succeeded in getting him out on bail. A grateful press filled its pages and airwaves with the story. Within a week Susan was taking the psychological tests that would establish that she was unfit to stand trial.

"Temporary insanity," Amos Cadbury said, lifting his snow-white brows. "Temporary."

When Father Dowling visited Susan the first time, she refused to talk to him. Even so, he spoke to her softly of divine mercy, planting a seed he hoped would take root. As if in confirmation of Tetzel's heated series, Susan seemed almost relieved to have been caught. Her confession had been detailed. She had availed herself of two keys to Stanley's car, one taken from Phyllis, the other from the office, both of which she had returned.

"Why did she do that?" Amos wondered.

"Ask Tetzel."

Amos made an impatient noise.

They were seated in the dining room of the rectory, and now Marie came in with the food, eliciting unstinted anticipatory praise from the venerable lawyer. Amos understood that Marie was not to be told of Father Dowling's role in the hiring of Parker the private investigator.

"It had to be one or the other of them," Marie said.

"How do you mean?" Amos asked.

"Phyllis Collins or Susan Sawyer. Imagine, having an affair with her husband's partner." Marie shook her head at the folly of mankind. "Well, *cherchez la femme.*"

"I thought you suspected David Jameson, Marie."

She looked patiently at Father Dowling. "He would never have the nerve."

David Jameson had informed Father Dowling at great length that he no longer aspired to be a permanent deacon. "My volunteer work in the senior center more than satisfies my pastoral instinct."

He was now engaged to Bridget, and it was as a concession to her friend that Edna suffered the Wednesday presence of Jameson in the center.

"Most of the people he tries to counsel want to talk about their teeth."

"Wisdom teeth?"

Edna ignored the remark. Wise woman.

After Susan was institutionalized, George Sawyer and Phyllis went off on a cruise together.

"I hope there's a chaplain aboard," Marie said.

"Ship captains can perform wedding ceremonies," Father Dowling said.

"What good is that?"

Since the Sawyers did not intend to remain in Fox River, Father Dowling did not tell Marie of the nuptial Mass he had said for Phyllis and George in the chapel of the Athanasian Fathers. Counseled, it seemed, by Jameson, George had obtained a scandalously rapid anullment. Whatever his personal thoughts on that, Father Dowling did not choose to be more Catholic than the Church and had agreed to preside at the wedding. Marie assumed he had gone off for his monthly day of recollection. He did have some time for recollection after the happy couple drove away.

The one person who seemed genuinely moved by the deaths of Stanley Collins and Bob Oliver was Shirley Escalante. She was closing up the agency office when Father Dowling visited her. On her desk was a framed photograph of herself and Bob Oliver, a gift from Sylvia Woods. Phyllis had been enriched by these tragic events, and George Sawyer had joined his insurance money to her fortune. Would they live happily ever after? Bridget and David Jameson were in the process of planning an elaborate wedding at which Father Dowling would preside. Only Shirley seemed devastated by events.

She sat behind her desk, surrounded by the cartons she had filled from the contents of the file cabinet. She seemed a widow of sorts.

"What will you do now, Shirley?"

She looked at Father Dowling with moist eyes.

"I can't afford a cruise." She tried to laugh. "It doesn't make much sense, but I will miss working here."

"Are you looking for another position?"

"Oh I have several offers. I'll be all right."

And she would be. Father Dowling was sure of it. She had returned to the religion of her fathers as if stimulated by the perfidy of her former employers. The communion of saints is a communion of sinners, too, repentant sinners. Loyal, efficient Shirley Escalante was one clear beneficiary of what had happened as she presided over the requiem of the Realtor for whom she had worked.